THE PIRATE
OF WORLD'S END

BOOKS BY LIN CARTER

THE GONDWANE EPIC

The Warrior of World's End
The Enchantress of World's End
The Immortal of World's End
The Pirate of World's End

ZARKON, LORD OF THE UNKNOWN:

The Nemesis of Evil
Invisible Death
The Volcano Ogre
The Earth Shaker

OTHER TITLES:

Beyond the Gates of Dream
The Black Star
The City Outside the World
Kellory the Warlock
The Man Who Loved Mars
The Quest of Kadji
Time War
Tower at the Edge of Time
Tower of the Medusa
The Wizard of Zao

THE PIRATE OF WORLD'S END

LIN CARTER

WILDSIDE PRESS
BERKELEY HEIGHTS • NEW JERSEY

THE PIRATE OF WORLD'S END

Wildside Press
P.O. Box 45
Gillette, NJ 07933-0045
www.wildsidepress.com

Cover art by Vincent Di Fate

FIRST WILDSIDE PRESS EDITION:
JANUARY 2001

Contents

Foreword: *A Redactorial Induction*

Book One

THE TALKING HEADS OF SOORM

1.	The Desolation of Oj	13
2.	Dalassa the Urgovian	21
3.	The Magnate Borgo Methrix	29
4.	Death by Howling	37
5.	Decline and Fall in Soorm	44

Book Two

PIRATES OF ZELPHODON

6.	Defenders One, Invaders Nothing	53
7.	Zarcas the Zirian	61
8.	Curious Custom of Korscio	68
9.	Zork Aargh Comes Aboard	76
10.	The Ookaboolaponga on the Warpath	83

Book Three

SILVERMANE ON ARJIS ISLE

11.	Horrog Makes Trouble	93
12.	Zollobus Spills the Beans	101
13.	Economics of Raschid	108

| 14. | Ganelon Silvermane Decides | 115 |
| 15. | Ishgadara Gets Impatient | 122 |

Book Four

THE GREAT ZIRIAN INVASION

16.	Resolving the Dilemma	131
17.	On the High Seas	138
18.	Lost and Found	144
19.	Palensus Choy Intervenes	152
20.	Hail and Farewell	160

Appendix: *Glossary of Places Mentioned in the Text* 167

A REDACTORIAL INDUCTION

THE Gondwane Epic is the last of Old Earth's major literary productions, and was completed in the Twilight of Time during the Eon of the Silver Phoenix. Its author or authors are unknown.

Such was the popularity, indeed the fame, of the epic that no fewer than forty-one commentaries were written upon the text of the epic over the successive eleven thousand years which followed its completion. Some of these are every bit as long as the epic itself, which is divided into ten books and comprises a sum total of more than six hundred thousand words.

In deciding to attempt a prose redaction of the epic I was fully sensitive to the enormity of the task and the intricacy of it. Translation is perhaps the least regarded of the arts, and certainly the most difficult; and to interpret properly the matter of the epic for readers of another eon required constant attention and explanation, some of which I have interpolated into the text, some given in footnotes, the remainder in various appendices.

At this point—the opening of the Fifth Book—we have arrived at midpoint. It seems appropriate here to indite a brief précis of that which has gone before:

Ganelon Silvermane, a Construct of the Time Gods, emerged from the Ardelix Vault beneath the Crystal Mountains before his appointed time, with his mind a blank but fully developed in the body. Adopted by an itinerant godmaker and his wife, one of the Pseudowomen of Chuu—Phlesco and Imminix—he demonstrated quite early his prowess when he defeated the rampaging Indigon herds at

Uth. He was then for a time tutored by a distinguished magician, the Illusionist of Nerelon, before commencing his adventures. Taken prisoner by the Death Dwarves, and by them delivered to their mistress, the Red Enchantress, he met during his brief captivity in Shai one Grrff the Xombolian, a Karjixian Tigerman, and a little boy named Phadia, who later became a disciple of the above magician. Between them they managed to—for a time at least—end the menace which the Enchantress posed to Silvermane's homeland and the realms around.

The Airmasters of Sky Island they next disposed of, leaving only the dreaded Warlord of the Ximchak Horde on the Illusionist's agenda of villains to be dispatched. Before his encounter could take place, however, the Illusionist returned to Nerelon where long-overdue business awaited his attentions. Silvermane continued his journey with Grrff, accompanied by Xarda, a girl knight of Jemmerdy. In the Mobile City of Kan Zar Kan they made the acquaintance of Kurdi, a bright and likable gypsy boy of the Iomagoths. The city itself they employed to destroy the Ximchaks who were then laying siege to Prince Erigon's city of Valardus. The siege ended, the city departed, and Erigon and Xarda wed, while Silvermane, Kurdi and Grrff—together with their new companions, Palensus Choy and Ollub Vetch, an immortal magician and his inventor friend—and a flying sphinxess named Ishgadara ventured north to defend Trancore against the ubiquitous Ximchaks. There Silvermane was convinced by Wolf Turgo, a Ximchak chieftain, to surrender to the Horde, since only by that means could he hope to effect the freedom of the Tigerman and the lady sphinx, who had been carried into Gompery (then suffering under a Ximchak occupation) following a battle.

In Gompland Silvermane was forced into servitude by Zaar the Warlord, but enlisted in one of the Ximchak clans, rapidly rose to prominence, and in time, besting Zaar in a duel to a death, actually replaced him as Warlord. Pitying the downtrodden Gomps, Ganelon restored Princess Ruzara to the throne and led the Horde out of Gompia on a lengthy and interminable overland journey across the northern parts of the Supercontinent.

In the Merdingian Regnate the Horde eventually decided to settle, some taking service as mercenaries to the various Regnatorial cities, others reverting to the nomadic hunting life of their ancestors. Ganelon relinquished his office as Warlord, and, with Grrff, Kurdi and Ishgadara commenced a long journey south, hoping eventually to find his way home to the Hegemony.

At the beginning of the Fifth Book of the Epic, to which I have given the title of *The Pirate of World's End,* it is exactly five years, four months and eleven days since Ganelon Silvermane emerged prematurely from the Time Vault beneath the ruins of Ardelix. He still does not know the full extent of the supernormal powers which the Time Gods instilled within their synthetic Construct.

Neither has he as yet the slightest inkling of the purpose for which he was bred.

So come—join me now at World's End in the Twilight of Time, as Ganelon Silvermane begins a new cycle of adventures on Gondwane the Great, Old Earth's last and mightiest continent.

—LIN CARTER

Book One

THE TALKING HEADS OF SOORM

The Scene: Lower Arzenia; the Desolation of Oj; Urgoph City; The Land of Soorm; The Hills of the Holy Heads.

The Characters: Ganelon Silvermane, Kurdi, Grrff the Xombolian, Ishgadara the Gynosphinx; Princess Dalassa; the Grand Magnate Borgo Methrix; Urgovians, Deacons, Guardsmen and Priests; Some Very Unexpected Pirates.

1.

THE DESOLATION OF OJ

Late in the afternoon of a year toward the end of the Eon of the Falling Moon, a peculiar party of travelers could be discerned as they traversed the wastelands of Lower Arzenia.

The first thing that was peculiar about these adventurers was that they were neither riding nor walking: they were *flying*. In the nearly seven hundred million years that have passed between our own age and that in which my tale is laid, the art of aeronautics had largely been lost, together with many of the physical sciences. The travelers were not, however, flying in any manner of sky vehicle, but bestride the broad and furry shoulders of an enormous and winged female sphinx.

Her name was Ishgadara and she was the property of a friendly magician called Palensus Choy. It was the harmless conceit of this sorcerer to beguile the tedium of his magically prolonged life by collecting a menagerie of beasts commonly thought mythical or, at very least, fabulous. Some of his specimens he found living in the remoter and wilder portions of the super-continent; others he was forced to create and nurture in his breeding vats. The Gynosphinx belonged to the latter category.

In order to make her actually capable of flight, Palensus Choy had had to increase her proportions somewhat beyond those to which art and mythology had assigned her species. Thrice the size of any lion Old Earth had borne in its prime, she had an immensely broad chest and shoulders whose massive thews would have looked more proper upon an elephant. These were required in order to anchor to her bones the muscles for her wings. When fully extended, they measured thirty-two feet from tip to tip, those wings, and their feathers were dark brown tipped with gold.

She had a thick mane of fleecy gold that curled about her neck and shoulders in a fashion thoroughly lionlike; but her enormous pink-nippled breasts were similar to those of a human female, and so were her features. Although her face was broader and larger and flatter than a woman's, her physiognomy was essentially feminine and human, with pinkish-white skin, large eyes of luminous green under a flat brow, a long flattened nose like a lion's muzzle but unwhiskered, and a broad grin which revealed blunt, strong tusks.

The rest of her was lionlike and clad in tawny, sandcolored fur. From the tip of her nose to the tip of her tail, she was nearly fifteen feet long.

Bestride her back, seated between her wings, sat a young gypsy boy named Kurdi. He was dark, with flashing bright eyes and tousled curls, and wore a skimpy tunic that left his brown thighs bare. An orphan, the lad had attached himself to the party of adventurers as a sort of combination squire, page, servant and general factotum. He had been about eleven then; now he was something more than thirteen and a half, with long legs and a cheerful, chirping voice beginning to break at unexpected times.

Seated behind the boy was a towering giant of a man, his naked hide tanned darkly bronze, his hair a long glittering name of metallic silver. He was immense, superbly muscular as a young gladiator; his magnificent body, which he indifferently bared to the chill winds, was clothed only in a war harness of black leather and boots. Over his shoulders a leather baldric supported a mighty broadsword: other than this he was unarmed.

His name was Ganelon Phlescosson, called Silvermane, and he was by now a warrior hero with a considerable reputation in several parts of the continent. He had emerged victorious from many battles and had overcome many adversaries, winning many honors. The Hegemonic cities had proclaimed him Hero of Uth; King Yemple had made him a Defender of Kan Zar Kan; he was a Knight of Valardus and a Baron of Trancore; and, until just recently he had been Chieftain of the Kuzak tribe, and Warlord of the Ximchak Horde.

His features were clean-shaven, grim, impassive, handsome in a way but peculiarly blank. Under scowling brows, his black eyes were magnetic. Women found him attractive, probably because of the sheer virility he radiated; but he had no experience with women, had Ganelon Silvermane.

Although he seemed fully grown and mature, he was actually only about five years old. That is to say, he had emerged from the Ardelix Vault only five years, four months and eleven days before. He had, of course, emerged from the entropy-null chamber fully grown.

Emotionally, he was still prepubescent, which explains, I think, why he had no interest as yet in women.

He was not a True Human, but an android, a synthetic man, a Construct bred by the mysterious Time Gods for a purpose yet unknown.

And seated behind Silvermane was the fourth and last of this peculiar party—and by no means the least peculiar of them all. I refer to Grrff the Xombolian, a Tigerman from Karjixia. To picture Grrff, you need only imagine a Bengal tiger who walks on his hind legs like a man and is capable of manlike speech, thought and emotion.

Beneath his striped orange and black and white hide there beat a heart fully capable of love and loyalty and courage.

Such was Grrff.

Six months before, the adventurers had left the encampments of the Ximchak Horde in a country to the north called the Merdingian Regnate.

For a time they had veered east to avoid the White Waste, which was thickly infested by the Vroych. The Vroych resemble scorpions grown to the size of alligators and painted purple, splotched with canary yellow. Vicious, nasty, mean-tempered, and extremely venomous are the Vroych; travelers generally avoid the bone-strewn Waste if at all possible.

Traveling east, the adventurers had skirted Hosh and the borders of Sorabdazon before crossing Poison River into Glundal country. They had flown over the Vermilion Marshes and had paused only briefly at Osch and Vemblem and Ardoza to take on fresh supplies.

They had not cared to visit Drudth for reason of the atrocious Custom they follow in Drudth.

Neither had they paused in Czinca, where men worship serpents; nor in Pirscoign, where there are no females and men mate with limber boys; nor in Foresco, where it is forbidden to have any hair.

But they did rest in Volesce, where the caravans loiter before attempting the passage over the Tucsan Mountains. In fact, they spent the winter there as guests of the Volescian Suzerain, one Farnoukh IV, an affable if trinocular gentleman whose skin coloring suggested he was in the terminal stages of food-poisoning.* A kindly, convivial old gentleman, the Suzerain loved nothing more than good, rip-snorting stories of excitement, adventure and derring-do. So, all winter long, Ganelon and Grrff kept their host happily entertained by recounting some of their deeds, exploits and recent journeys.

Crossing the mountains with spring, they had encountered a bothersome adventure on the Harth Plains: a raiding party of Vurble slavers had carried off Grrff, and it had taken his friends several weeks to find him and to effect his rescue. These slavers pursue their abominable trade from hot-air balloons and customarily dip down over campfires at night and snatch up one or another likely-looking prospect in their collapsible nets, carrying them off to a mountaintop aerie called Hoyk, whose peak is reputedly unsealable, having been polished as slick as glass by several thousand generations of Vurbles.

They encountered no troubles along the mighty Kurge, whose gliding floods are home to quaint raft-built Floating Towns. Neither did any attempt to molest them on Zynor Island. And they flew over the Rapids of Ulkh rather than attempt to run them: the Ulkh Wreckers, who infest that portion of the Kurge, waved futile fists and hooted obscenities at them as they flapped lazily by overhead bestride Ishgadara.

For five days now they had been traversing the wastelands, having by this point in their southerly journey crossed the borders from Upper into Lower Arzenia.

These wastelands were known as the Desolation of Oj, and caravans never attempted their crossing if it could be helped. (Perhaps I should interpolate at this point the explanation that at the border just beyond the Rapids, the enormous Kurge enters a cavern and traverses the ensuing forty or fifty leagues underground, before emerging to the surface again to empty into the Inland Sea.)

At the moment the travelers were debating as to where to land for the night. They had treated the Desolation with gin-

---

* A sub-branch of the Lesser Illyriath Yarglargs of the neighboring Conglomerate of Inner Pongolia to the west, the Volescians have three eyes in their foreheads, and are of the color of cooked spinach.

gerly respect thus far, assuming that if the merchant caravans avoided the rocky sand-strewn waste, as they habitually did, it was for good reason. The avarice of merchants being as common to Ganelon's time as to our own era, there was doubtless a core of solid sensibleness to this argument. Nevertheless, land they must, for the Gynosphinx could not continue to fly all night, having already flown all day. And the travelers were increasingly aware of an acute need to relieve nature.

Ganelon—whose eyesight was considerably superior to any True Man's—spotted a low, flat-topped mesa dead ahead which looked bare and easily defensible. In his deep, somber voice he called this feature to the attention of his companions, modestly recommending the miniature plateau as his own choice for their camping place.

They landed shortly thereafter, and Kurdi hopped off first, eager to stretch his long legs. The next to dismount was Grrff the Xombolian, who had taken aboard too frequent doses of liquid refreshment during the long, boring flight. The discomfort of his kidneys was evidently extreme, for, wearing an expression of disgruntled dignity, the Tigerman went trotting off to relieve himself behind the nearest boulder with swift dispatch.

The crest of the mesa was a bare tableland of dry rock littered with crumbling stones and boulders and with, here and there, patches of black sand wind-blown into stony pockets. No living thing apparently made the mesa its home; and there was nothing that grew here, either, from which Grrff might have been able to fuel a fire. Perforce they must devour their rations cold, washed down with red Ximchak wine and water.

While the boy Kurdi laid out the meal picnic-fashion on a large cloth, and Ishgadara groomed her weary wings with a huge wet tongue like a pink flannel washrag, Ganelon and the Karjixian strolled about a bit, exploring.

"Where do you think we be, anyhow, big man?" asked Grrff in his hoarse, gruff voice—wherein just the faintest trace of a tiger's growl could be discerned.

Silvermane shrugged. "Getting close to Soorm, I should think. A bit farther on south, it must be. But we can't very well miss it. It's this side of the Inland Sea."

It was the intent of the adventurers to turn east when they reached the edges of the sea, so as to fly directly into South-

ern YamaYamaLand. They had no maps and no compass to
guide them, and the stars and constellations in these latitudes
were unfamiliar to them. They really wanted to be in
Northern YamaYamaLand, but had to go the long way about
because their knowledge of these parts of Gondwane the
Great—old Earth's last and greatest continent—consisted of
vague report, idle rumor, sheer hearsay, and downright fabri-
cation.

They were on their way home, more or less. Ganelon's
home was the city of Zermish in the Hegemony; it was there
that his foster parents, Phlesco the Godmaker and Imminix
the pseudowoman, lived; Grrff's homeland, Karjixia, lay a
trifle farther north. They had both been away for years on
their travels: now, after fatiguing adventures in far, exotic
lands, they felt a nostalgic yearning for familiar streets and
faces.

As for Kurdi, the little Iomagothic boy had adopted the
two of them in place of the father he had never known. But
of the two he rather loved Ganelon the more, and had long
since chosen to accompany the giant Construct wherever he
might choose to venture. Ishgadara was sort of "on loan" to
Silvermane and the Tigerman; eventually, they supposed, she
would fly back home to Zaradon, the Flying Castle atop
Mount Naroob, where she lived with her master, Palensus
Choy. Or perhaps in time Choy would fly thither in Zaradon
to pick her up, when it became obvious that neither Ganelon
nor the Tigerman had any further need of the sphinx-girl as
an aerial steed.

"Know anything about Soorm?" inquired the Xombolian
after a time.

"Not much," admitted the other. "Enough to suggest we fly
over it rather than ride through it, though."

"That's where they got them Talking Heads," mused the
Tigerman, rubbing his whiskery jowls with one huge paw.
"Never knew what they meant by 'em, but all his life ol'
Grrff's heard tell of the Talking Heads o' Soorm. . . ."

"Me, too," muttered Silvermane, a bit uncomfortably. He
did not like the sound of the phrase; no, not at all.

In this remote age of the immeasurably distant future, the
few dwindling remnants of True Men shared the vastness of
the super-continent with many new forms of life, some of
them manlike and intelligent (like the Tigermen of Karjixia),
but most of them as distinctly unlike men as it is possible to

be. And in their travels both Ganelon Silvermane and his friend Grrff had encountered more than a few of these.

Most recently, there had been an adventure up north in Pardoga with the Strange Little Men of the Hills—an adventure from which the enormous Ximchak Horde had narrowly escaped destruction to the last scarlet-eyed barbarian warrior.

For the Strange Little Men were a rare form of animate mineral, and were quite unkillable.

Earlier, before his travelings had begun, Ganelon had fought the powerful and dangerous Indigons, whose herds had come marauding down to imperil the Hegemony.

Nor did he recall without a shudder the Ghost-Phexians, those immaterial specters who lived trapped within the solidity of the Crystal Mountains, but who could drive one mad.

Nor, for that matter, the Death Dwarves, prodigious strong little monsters who ate poison and were a form of Antilife.

If the Talking Heads of Soorm were anything like these other uncanny brutes and monstrosities, he would just as soon fly at a comfortable altitude above their domain, than pass through on foot.

They dined frugally on cold meats, mint jellies, dried fruits, tough yellow bread, water and wine.

The sun sank below the western horizon of Gondwane in a blazon of vermilion and tangerine and two other colors, but newly added to the spectrum, to which our senses are not attuned.*

The stars came forth in regal splendor, like diamonds sewn upon the velvet gowns of empresses.

As they rolled themselves into their cloaks for the night, the dark landscape was flooded by an uncanny silver brilliance. Above the horizon floated a titanic orb which filled a very sizable portion of the sky. A tremendous disc of pinkish silver it was, with features common to the moon of our own day, but of proportions stupendously larger.

It was the Falling Moon.

Over the span of hundreds of millions of years, the drag of Old Earth's gravitational attraction had gradually slowed the forward flight of her ancient companion, until the moon was drawn nearer and nearer to the earth so that she bulked with ominous hugeness in her nocturnal skies.

---

* The Sixth Commentary on the epic opines that these are hao and wanine, the two colors in the infra-red end of the spectrum which are immediately adjacent to the octave of visible light as we of today know it.

Some said the moon would eventually fall, crushing the world.

Others prophesied that at some indefinable point the strain of conflicting forces would tear the moon apart, raining meteors like mountain ranges upon the world, destroying all life. Indeed, black zigzag cracks defaced the gleaming surface, easily visible to the unaided eye.

Grrff and Ganelon and Ishgadara and Kurdi had seen that titanic and threatening spectacle every night of their lives, and fell asleep without concern for future destruction.

When they awoke with dawn, however, Kurdi was not there.

2.

DALASSA THE URGOVIAN

There was no sign of a struggle that either Ganelon or Grrff could perceive. The boy's cloak lay open, crumpled, and still warm from the heat of his body. The gritty sand around the place where he had slept did not seem particularly disturbed. There were no footprints.

Grrff glared skywards, hackles raised along his furry nape, black lips writhing back from sharp white fangs.

"Vurble slavers come this far south, you s'pose?" he growled. The memory of how easily the balloon-riding raiders had netted him still rankled; to have been so absurdly captured was a humiliation which the burly Karjixian would not soon forget.

Ganelon shook his head. It had been months since they had left the Harth Plains, and they had been traveling steadily ever since.

"Me go looking for liddle poy, hokay?" queried Ishgadara hopefully. Sphinxess or no, her motherly heart had warmed to the mischievous, playful lad; the thought of Kurdi in trouble, maybe even in danger, upset her and made her want to break heads.

Grrff and Silvermane felt much the same way, and were as anxious to ascertain what had happened to Kurdi as was the Gynosphinx. So, pausing only to snatch up their gear and bedding, they bundled everything into the saddlebags, slung them across the tawny furred haunches of the sphinx-girl, and ascended into the upper atmosphere for a quick aerial search.

21

"*There's* something!" grunted Grrff, pointing with his ygdraxel.

Ganelon looked, saw a dead ornith lying in a sand-filled gully on the southerly slopes of the little mesa on whose top they had camped for the night, and bade Ishgadara descend. Hopping off her back, the two warriors investigated.

The ornith, or ornithohippus, is a riding beast commonly used in these parts of Gondwane the Great during this eon as a mode of transportation. Beaked, feathered but wingless, it resembled a quadrupedal bird, with claws instead of hooves: like a curious cross between bird and horse it was, and about the size of the latter.

This particular specimen had not been a wild, but a tame, ornith. Ganelon pointed out how the saddle girths had worn smooth the feathery flanks of the dead animal. Grrff, for his part, found the cause of its demise: a light javelin or dart had transfixed the vitals of the creature.

The loose, soft sand about the animal's cadaver was violently disturbed. Other similar gullies nearby were filled with sand which lay smooth, sleeked by the wind. But here the sand was pocked and kicked about in sure and obvious signs of a struggle.

They searched the ground around for a bit longer, hunting for some clue as to what had transpired. Then Grrff uttered a growling cry and snatched from where it lay half-covered by the sand a smooth scarab-shape of slick ceramic, colored an eye-hurting shade of raw indigo.

Ganelon examined it, grimly. There was no doubt in the young giant's mind that this was the Ukwukluk talisman the lad habitually wore suspended about his throat by a thong. Indeed, the thong was still threaded through the slot which pierced the upper end of the amulet. It was broken, that thong.

Mounting Ishgadara, they flew off again, but this time lower in altitude, crossing low sandy hills and a brief expanse of desert, heading south. The claw-prints of many orniths had recently traversed this small waste, for their passage had disturbed the sand. They flew on in the direction the prints had seemed to indicate.

Before long Silvermane's keen sight discerned a sizable party ahead of them. It consisted of four very tall and lean men, wrapped in awning-striped desert robes with cowls drawn up shielding their faces from windblown sand, mount-

ed on orniths, and two other persons who were evidently
captives of the four, since their hands were bound behind
their backs and the reins of their beasts were tied to the sad-
dlehorns of the four robed riders.

One of the captives was a young girl with amazing hair of
bright gold, dressed in abbreviated bits of ornamental metal.

The other was Kurdi.

Like a thunderbolt, striking abruptly and without warning
from clear and sunny skies, the gigantic Gynosphinx fell into
the midst of these travelers, her strong bronze wings raising a
dust-haze. Ganelon, brandishing the glittering length of the
Silver Sword, and Grrff, wielding his Tigermanic ygdraxel,
came hurtling from the back of the lady sphinx, booming
their challenges.

With a thundering of "A Zermishman! A Zermishman!"
Ganelon leaped upon the nearest rider, who had frozen with
astonishment in the saddle, wide eyes gleaming whitely from
the shadow of his cowl. He swung the whistling blade and a
severed head (still fixed in an expression of bulge-eyed astonishment) went bouncing among the dunes like a coconut.

A strangled, gargling yowl from behind him suggested to
Ganelon that his Karjixian comrade had just disemboweled
one of the other riders with a well-placed thrust of his hook-
clawed weapon directly in the entrails. This was, in fact, the
case.

The two other riders, those who as yet remained unscathed,
hesitated for a fraction of a second, then cast back their
cowls to display gaunt, angry faces with shaven brows and
piercing black eyes. They seemed human enough, save that
they lacked anything resembling ears, and their chocolate
faces were hideously embellished with elaborate tattooing in
scarlet metallic inks. The tattooing was identical on each
bony, furious visage: like an overlay mask of scowling red
wires, outlining and (as it were) underscoring their dour,
down-turned mouths and heavily-frowning brows.

"Cease these gory depredations at once, heretical outland-
ers," snapped the first in a harsh voice. "You unwittingly in-
terfere in the holy business of consecrated Deacons."

"Aye, atheistical foreigners," chimed in the other with a
frosty glare. "Beware lest we invoke upon you the Howling
Curse! As holy officers of the Secular Arm we possess the
requisite degree of initiatehood—"

"Set your prisoners free and you may go your way," said

Silvermane stolidly, holding the Silver Sword at guard position.

"Impossible," sniffed the first Deacon. "The female is a runaway, chosen in the annual selection to serve the Carnate Ones—"

"A polite euphemism for temple prostitution," the girl remarked boldly from behind Silvermane. He glanced over his shoulder; both she and Kurdi had been gagged with strips of red cloth, but the gold-haired girl had evidently bitten through her gag with strong white teeth. Her clear-skinned, evenly-tanned features wore an expression desperate and yet resolute. The appeal in her eyes was unspoken, perhaps from pride, but eloquent. They were purple, those eyes. Ganelon thought her remarkably pretty.

He looked back to the first Deacon just in time to see the churchman with a thin-lipped snarl raise in one bony hand a lithe silver-handled whip of braided black leather. He was about to smite the blonde girl across the face for her temerity in speaking up so tartly.

The Silver Sword whistled through the hot air again, a mirror-bright blur, smudged with scarlet. Both whip and the hand holding it fell into the red-dabbled sand. Croaking a wordless cry, the Deacon bent over in the saddle, nursing the stump of his wrist which fountained scarlet drops.

"Perhaps we had best do as the heretic says, Deacon Ildth," murmured the other tattooed man, wetting his lips nervously. "We can always smite them with anathema later when they have gone," he added ingenuously. Groaning, Ildth nodded; the second Deacon got stiffly down from his mount, crossed to where the girl sat grinning, severed her bonds with a slim curved dirk, then tended to the boy.

Ganelon and the Tigerman watched impassively as this was done.

The fellow hesitated, watching Ganelon from the corner of his eye. Then: "The beasts, however, are clearly property of Mother Church: our share of the Tithe will be docked unless we return with all six orniths, which were checked out of the Temple Stables and must be returned forthwith."

"I'll keep this one to replace poor Trinka, whom you slew," said the girl sharply. Grrff chuckled; he liked a wench who spoke up for herself. Ganelon remained impassive, but he, too, admired the girl's spirit. She rather reminded him of Xarda, a companion of his earlier adventures.

"Your beast was slain while assisting you to transgress the

decision of the Carnate Ones," the second Deacon argued primly. "The beast, then, was attainted with your own heretical sin of Disobedience in the Second Degree, and its slaughter was a kindness. The Ninth Mysteriarch, in his tractate on Contagious Karma, clearly points out—"

"Oh, bother the Ninth Mysteriarch!" flared the girl hotly, tossing her bright curls. "*And* the Tenth, for all of that! I raised dear Trinka from the egg, and you killed her, you bloodless stone worshipper!"

"Let the runaway keep the beast, Pervwyn," said Ildth in a faint voice. "My maiming has dimmed my Aura so that I lack sufficient Mana to curse them with the Howling. Let us return to sanctified ground so that my healing may commence. Our brethren will, of course, deal out justice to these abominable sinners at another time."

"As you say, Ildth," agreed Pervwyn. "The Oracular Office can, of course, trace their whereabouts at leisure."

"No, you can take the two mounts," said Silvermane. "We will escort the young lady wherever she wishes to go on our own mount."

He obviously referred to Ishgadara. The two Deacons eyed the big sphinx-girl with acrid disapproval.

"The so-called sphinx is an invention of discredited mythologies, and it would be heretical in the first degree to acknowledge the existence of the phantasm," observed Ildth aloofly.

Ishgadara grinned hugely and flirted her strong wings, blowing gritty sand in his face. Paling, the wounded Deacon attempted to ignore the grit that stung his eyes.

"Whatever you say," growled Grrff, wearying of this palaver. "Just beat it out o' here, you two, and let us fly off on our phantasm." He grinned and guffawed loudly at the notion of flying off on something that did not exist.

The two Deacons gathered up the dead, tethered all six of the orniths* in line, and rode off into the southwest, the unharmed deacon assisting the other, who swayed weakly in the saddle.

Ganelon turned his attention to the girl, once he had scoured the gore from his glittering blade by plunging it a time or two to the hilt in the dry sand and replaced it in its sheath. Kurdi was babbling excited explanations.

---

* The First Commentary suggests that the sixth ornith was probably a pack beast, since the Soorm Priestarchy had no way of guessing they would capture Kurdi.

"Got up to—uh," the lad started, broke off, glanced shyly at the golden-haired girl, flushed, went on: "go behind a rock—*you* know! Looked over the edge an' saw this girl bein' chased by all them others—"

"Why didn't you wake us?" growled Grrf with mock ferocity, tousling the boy's head with a gentle cuff of one great paw.

"Fell over the edge," Kurdi admitted sheepishly. "Slid down ina sand an' they grabbed me, too. Gagged me, so's I *c'u'n't* yell."

"Well, thank Galendil you're not harmed," said Silvermane affectionately. He had been looking the blonde girl over with considerable approval.

She was tall for a young woman, and looked about twenty, with classically perfect features, slim, chiseled nostrils, and lush lips as pink and moist as sliced watermelon. Her warm golden tan and luxurious bright hair were set off richly by the skimpy garb she wore. Her lithe, smooth-skinned but voluptuous body was covered only by quaint ornaments of silver filigree: two small openwork shields clung to the tops of her full, firm breasts, each set with a flashing ruby to conceal her nipples; a small shield-shaped device, also of filigree silver wire, concealed her sex. These ornaments (they were hardly decent enough to be considered clothing) were held in place by woven cords of crimson silk. Her feet were shod in red silk slippers and her legs wore silver filigree greaves. The rest of her—and there was quite a *lot* of the rest of her—was gloriously, exuberantly, unabashedly nude.

"I am Ganelon, called Silvermane, a warrior of Zermish in the Hegemony," said that worthy—his mother had always told him to introduce himself politely in strange company. "This is my friend Grrff, a Tigerman out of Karjixia. Our companion, Kurdi, you have already met; how do you do?"

"I do quite a bit better, since you showed up, stranger," said the girl with a warm smile; for her part she was looking him up and down boldly, and liked what she saw. "What about your imaginary sphinx over there: don't I get an introduction to her, as well?"

"Me Ishy," said the Gynosphinx with a huge grin, waddling over to meet the golden girl. In her brief and rather sheltered life thus far, Ishgadara had met few females of the race of True Men, and never one so busty. She ogled the girl's nearly naked breasts with cheerful interest. "You got-um big tits like Ishy," the Gynosphinx observed.

Ganelon and Kurdi flushed crimson and Grrff snorted to keep from laughing. The blonde girl, however, seemed not at all affronted: in fact she threw back her head and laughed heartily. Then, glancing humorously down at Ishgadara's own enormous teats (each bigger than her own head), she shook her head, tears of laughter sparkling on her lashes.

"Not *quite*, thank Galendil!" Then, less amusedly, as if suddenly remembering her manners, she announced: "I am Dalassa, the second daughter and eleventh child of Borgo Methrix, Magnate of the First Rank, down in Urgoph. I must admit that I have never heard of Zermish or Karjixia, but as long as you dropped by when you did, for all I care you could hail from the Eleven Scarlet Hells of the Ting-a-Ling Mythos!"

"You're *awful* pretty," said Kurdi, breathlessly. He had been staring up at the voluptuous golden girl for some time, with wide, dreamy eyes.

Kurdi, you will recall, was by now thirteen and, obviously, of an age to notice beautiful young women—especially nearly naked ones. The girl winked and blew him a kiss and Kurdi flushed and dropped his eyes shyly.

They flew back to the mesa and brewed a pot of tea.

Fire blazed in the heaped, dry scrub they had gathered at the desert's edge. Fayowaddy tea simmered aromatically in a small iron pot. They munched a late, dry breakfast, washed down with the steaming tea, while they talked.

Urgoph, it seemed, was a port city on the northern shores of the Sea of Zelphodon which lay to the south not far away. Soorm, the land of whose borders they were transgressing, was a theocracy situated among the rocky hills of the desert country. Previously it had exerted no influence over the merchant princes, called Magnates, who ruled the seaport town. But within recent memory the priestarchy had insinuated its tentacles into the High Councils of Urgoph.

"Every year they hold a sort of festival now, wherein the most luscious of the nubile girls are selected to 'serve the Carnate Ones,'" said Dalassa, distastefully. "Which simply means that they become the concubines of the priests who are the servitors of the Talking Heads. I was unfortunate enough to be chosen in this year's festival; prior to this, my father had hidden me away among the low-caste serving girls when the Deacons came around. He would smudge my face with soot and make me walk with a limp."

"And *this* year?" asked Ganelon solemnly.

"This year they took us by surprise," said the blonde girl with a grimace.

"And this—ah—garment," he said, gesturing at her nearly unclothed self. "Is this the way the Soormian priests dress their temple prostitutes?"

"This?" said the girl, surprisedly, looking down at her smooth, golden body. "Why, this is the way all the women of Urgoph dress. If they are pretty enough to get away with it, that is."

"Um," said Ganelon Silvermane.

3.

THE MAGNATE BORGO METHRIX

Later that morning they flew on Ishy's back across the Desolation, traversing the land of Soorm, arriving at Urgoph in early afternoon.

It was a pleasant town of red-roofed houses, shops and mansions, sprawling in a crescent about the mouth of the Kurge. The huge river, one of the thirty which fed into the Inland Sea, had by that point emerged from its underground travels. ˙

Dalassa had talked all the way. The pleasantly uninhibited girl was a lively traveling companion; the novelty of her rescuers delighted her. She had met few travelers, for her birth had precluded her from mingling freely with the various merchants, pilgrims and assorted travelers who passed through Urgoph on their way to the several islands and archipelagoes of the sea.

The experience of flight thrilled her, and she egged Ishgadara into a series of blood-chilling swoops and figure eights and Immelmanns, before Ganelon sternly bade the lady sphinx cut out the nonsense and stick to a steady keel, as it were.

She chattered brightly with Grrff whom she thought of as a cuddly, talkable teddy bear. She flirted outrageously with Kurdi, who was in utter bliss. She even flirted, more demurely, with Ganelon, whom she thought magnificent.

In a word, she talked all the way home.

And when she got home, she found, much to her surprise, that nobody was there. Nobody at all.

During the time she had suffered training in the erotic arts under the tutelage of the holy eunuchs—before she climbed a drainpipe, purloined her favorite ornith, and rode off hopefully, toward freedom—it seemed, her father had been elected Grand Magnate of All the Urgovians, and had, naturally, moved into the Magnatorial Palace, selling his mansion to another.

Urgoph was a merchant city and the merchants were the ruling magistrates. Any man of wealth derived from the mercantile trades could become a Magnate, either of the Third, Second or First Rank. Her father had been of the First, until the ballot of his fellow merchants had elevated him to the princedom.

Which made her, now, a Princess.*

These facts were learned through interrogating the night watchman hired by the Magnate who had recently purchased the mansion but had not, as yet, moved in. Dalassa directed their flight to the palace of the Grand Magnate, and they were welcomed with open arms. Or at least she was.

Her father, the Grand Magnate, was an affable, cordial, rather corpulent man with ruddy, clean-shaven cheeks and splendid robes. (The women of Urgoph went mostly bare; the men were covered from nape to toe. Odd custom; but there it is.) He was delighted to see her, heartily relieved at her escape from the churchly bordello, warmly grateful to her heroic rescuers, and scared stiff at the prospect of getting in trouble with the Soormians.

However, his present rank made his palace more or less off limits to officers of the secular arm, save under extraordinary circumstances. He ordered a feast in their honor, and installed the adventurers in suites of the most sumptuous and luxurious appointments.

Silvermane relaxed in a foamy bath of scented waters, and reluctantly permitted his back to be scrubbed by giggling bevies of nubile slave girls. Fairly puritanical as far as relations between the sexes went, Silvermane was not particularly scandalized by nudity. The contradiction in his makeup was one of those little things that make people uniquely interesting.

* Actually, her title was Munificentessa. Her father was His Munificence, the Grand Magnate. Urgoph was, you see, another oligarchy, like Gompland.

Kurdi loved the bath, and pinched the rounded bottoms of the girls whenever Ganelon did not seem to be watching.

Grrff, descended from catlike ancestors, had a catlike antipathy to bathing at all. So, in his case, the slave girls groomed him all over with a steel currycomb while he relaxed, purring, under their ministrations. Then they oiled his fur with scented balsams.

Ishgadara, too enormous to fit any bathtub, wallowed and splashed in a rooftop cistern, then let the girls rub her down and oil her wings. (They also teased her golden mane into fat sausage curls and painted her claws scarlet. She didn't mind.)

The feast that night was interminable, an affair of thirty-nine courses: nine soups, nine stews or ragouts, nine dishes of meat or fish or fowl, nine varieties of salad, and three pastry or fruit desserts. Washed down with eleven different wines, sherbets, brandies and piping-hot tea. Delicious.

They slept like the dead, hugely enjoying the hammock-beds of the Urgovians, and the perfume of the scented night candles. Grrff didn't care if they *ever* left Urgoph.

A number of slave girls drifted through Ganelon's suite before he retired, ostensibly on this or that errand, but actually to be available in case he desired to sleep with one of them.

Some were blondes, brunettes or redheads; others were shaven bald or wore elaborate wigs tinted fantastic colors. They were of all ages, from eleven to thirty, and all shapes, from boy-slim to *zaftig* plump. And they were dressed in all manner of intriguing raiment, formal gowns, transparent lacy shifts, briefs, leather or metal or glass pieced together, and more than a few of them were completely naked. (Some wore only body paint, while a few were tattooed from head to foot, and one statuesque beauty had been entirely gilded.)

Ganelon dismissed them all and finally got up and barred the door so that he could get some sleep.

Kurdi, who slept next door, was offered no such nubile enticements, much to his disappointment. The male age of consent in Urgoph was fourteen—unlucky for him.

There being no Tigerwomen in the city, Grrff was similarly left alone. That was all right with him, although he had a healthy appetite for bouncy bed pleasure: males of his race were excited to copulation only by the odors of Tigermanic females in heat.

Dalassa stayed up late, arguing with her father. She had a healthy respect for the oracular powers of the Soormians, while her paternal parent tended to pooh-pooh, with unshaken aplomb, their reputed ability to see through walls. Borgo Methrix' point was that the only thing they had to fear was a spy or informer. Dalassa felt the Oracular Office could trace them here with ease, and that with dawn a posse of Deacons would be pounding on the door.

Borgo listened to her closely, but tended generally to discount her warnings as the ravings of a feminine hysteria. The plump, smooth-faced man truly loved his daughter and regretted the inroads the Soormians had made, in recent years, into the sovereignity of Urgoph. A born politician, Borgo saw his position as a delicate one: to maintain, discreetly, the balance of power between the Chamber of Magnates and the meddlesome priests. This was to be done with soothing words, amenable edicts, tact, diplomacy and, where possible, outright bribery.

His stiff-necked predecessor, Whillix IV, had fallen by an unwise policy of inflexible refusal to negotiate. "Negotiate" was Borgo's middle name, and just about summed up his political career. When Dalassa had been taken away by the priests, he had worked tirelessly for her freedom, with bribery, intimidation and selective assassination, not to mention a spot or two of sheer blackmail. Luckily, the girl had gotten away on her own.

This family council was attended by all of Dalassa's siblings. Her brothers, Jarvith, Orgad, Hovo and Yannuch, sided with their father in a policy of conciliation, concealment and complacency. Her sisters, Vangarda and Ivivriana, sided with her that it was unlikely they could hide her and her rescuers from the priests. Her tweenies—the Urgovians, not quite. as human as they looked, had *three* sexes—Lakmu, Dulachath, Nahham and Fenodryia, believed that she should flee into the islands of the Sea.

The council ended on a stalemate. It was nearly dawn, anyway.

And by morning they were in trouble. Deacons were, as Dalassa had predicted, pounding at the gate.

So were thirty of the Civic Guard.

The Guardsmen were unhappy at their temerity in, as it were, bearding their very own Grand Magnate in his den. But the Deacons had insisted, the Writ for Search and Seizure was properly signed, and there were nine Temple Proctors along to see the Guardsmen did their duty.

The Majordomo of the Palace, one Pynox Tethri, ushered

them into the Third Lesser Audience Chamber. In a few moments Borgo himself came waddling in, his corpulence wrapped in a mauve velvet morning robe. He looked short of temper; he also looked just a bit apprehensive—and despised himself for it.

The leader of the search party, Senior Deacon Yinth, cleared his throat and began reading the Writ at rapid-fire pace. All formalities and legalese aside, it baldly accused Borgo Methrix of harboring a runaway fugitive, namely his own daughter, and her accomplices.

Borgo purpled and compressed his lips together on the explosion he longed to vent. Senior Deacon Yinth, a hachet-faced old crow of a man, fixed him with a cold yet burning eye.

"Do not think to fabricate or prevaricate, Grand Magnate!" he rasped frostily. "The heretics escaped bestride a flying beast: the identical creature was seen at earliest dawn soaring up from the rooftops of your own Magnatorial Palace. I have forty-two eye-witnesses to this event, including, *harrumph*, myself."

The color drained from the plump features of Borgo Methrix; he looked harried. If this were true, then it would be idle for him to pretend that his daughter Dalassa and her protectors had not arrived yesterday.

And it must be admitted here that Senior Deacon Yinth had the facts perfectly straight. It was the pleasant habit of Ishgadara to enjoy an early morning flight when she woke up, just to stretch her wings. She was, even at that moment, soaring in lazy circles high above the town.

Knowing it was hopeless did not make it any easier for Borgo Methrix. He determined to tough it out. Fixing the Deacon with a bland, candid eye he assumed an expression of unruffled calm. And, when he spoke, his voice was slightly irritated but otherwise composed.

"The last I saw of my second-eldest daughter and eleventh child, Senior Deacon," he announced with the serenity of one whose conscience is clear and untainted, "was when, garland-wreathed but otherwise stark naked, she was led off in the triumphal procession to the Temple Precincts. If she has since returned to my home, it is not within my knowledge. Indeed, she could hardly have done so, since during her service to the Carnate Ones, she could not have known of the swift elevation of her father's rank, nor that the House of the Methrixi had been sold to the House of the

Hnanthae and that her former family have taken up residence in the Grand Magnatorial Palace."

"The beast—" snapped the Senior Deacon, but Borgo cut him off with a lifted palm.

"I am not to be held responsible for the comings or goings of beasts," he said with unruffled aplomb.

Obviously fuming, the Deacon glared at him with icy malignance; the Magnate returned his look indifferently, as if unconcerned by these accusations.

"In that case, doubtless the Grand Magnate will have no objections if the palace is searched?" said Yinth cunningly.

"No objection whatsoever," returned Methrix suavely. The Civic Guardsmen, under the watchful eye of the Proctors, immediately began a search of the palace. They had apparently consulted the original plans of the building, which had been constructed toward the beginning of the present epoch, for they knew every chamber, suite, stair and passage.

Borgo took his breakfast in the Audience Chamber under the cold, accusatory eye of the Senior Deacon. The Magnate maintained his composure with considerable effort of will, and ate with what appeared to be good appetite, occasionally regarding the fretful Deacon with looks of bored unconcern. Inwardly, of course, he was knotted with tension and could never in after days recall what it was that he had eaten: it *tasted* like sawdust, but probably wasn't.

It took the Guardsmen about three hours to search the enormous and rambling palace. Ordinarily, it would have taken about an hour and a half, but, finding nothing in the way of incriminating evidence, they searched the building twice at the Senior Deacon's insistence.

Reluctantly—grudgingly—even he was forced at length to conclude the runaways were not at present housed in the palace. Although how they could have eluded the searchers or escaped from the building, which was heavily cordoned off, was beyond Yinth.

As he left he turned to fire one parting shot.

"You have not heard the last of this, Grand Magnate," he said with venom.

"Indeed?" shrugged Borgo Methrix, cocking one brow nonchalantly. "I rather fancy that I have. At any rate, a good morning to Your Deaconship."

With a derisive snort and a bitter scowl Yinth left, escorted by the grinning Guardsmen (more than a few of whom saluted the Magnate with a wink as they trooped out) and sour-looking Proctors.

Borgo collapsed with a whoosh of long-pent breath, loudly called for unmixed wine, and roared for his Majordomo. The drink and Pynox Tethri appeared simultaneously, the one carrying the other (and I give my readers leave to figure out which).

"Where, in the name of Great Gux, did you *hide* them?" demanded Borgo Methrix after taking aboard a good pint of strong blue wine.

Pynox favored his master with a conspiratorial leer. "In the kitchens."

"The kitchens? The *kitchens?* Why, they searched the kitchens twice, you fool!" rumbled the Magnate.

"Yes, Your Munificence, they did. But they didn't think of looking in the pots—"

"In the *pots?*" exclaimed Borgo Methrix incredulously. "Why—why—you can't hide fully grown persons in kitchen pots, you gibbering lout!"

"Ah, but I beg to differ with Your Munificence on *that* point," smirked the Majordomo with an oily grin. "For you indeed can . . . if the pots are as big as these palace pots, that is."

Borgo Methrix opened his mouth to give voice to an incoherent roar, then shut it, reflecting. There were one hundred and eighty-seven individuals currently residing within the Magnatorial Palace. Besides the Magnate's family and concubines, there were secretaries, archivists, heralds, butlers, maids, cooks, housekeepers, courtiers, various officials, grooms, stable-boys, chefs, messengers and Galendil-only-knew who else. And the pots used in the kitchens of the palace to feed this assemblage were enormous covered cauldrons. . . .

Yes, it was quite possible, he concluded upon mature reflection.

"*Kerrumph!* Very well, then. Good work, my man: quick thinking, 'pon my word."

"I thank Your Munificence kindly. However, in all honesty, it was an idea conceived by the Munificentessa herself, and not a notion of mine own," said Pynox.

A faint smile tugged at the corners of Borgo Methrix' lips.

"It was, eh? *Her* idea, you say! Clever girl; takes after her sainted mother, you know," he said with a chuckle. Then, as the picture of Ganelon Silvermane and Grrff the Xombolian and his own princess of a daughter clambering into greasy kitchen pots formed within his mind, he began to laugh, his numerous chins and cheeks wobbling in rhythm to the spasms of hilarity, and his impressive paunch rippling thereto.

A good joke on that sour old Deacon. But—how long before the seers of Soorm turned the joke on *him?*

4.

DEATH BY HOWLING

The Magnate Borgo Methrix was unhappy about it, but the calm reason in the arguments presented by Ganelon Silvermane won him over.

In his heart, Dalassa's father knew very well that the only solution to their present predicament was for his daughter and her new-found friends to leave Urgoph, and that quickly.

"The longer we stay here, sir, the greater the danger to your own position, power and prestige," said Silvermane solemnly. Methrix snorted rudely.

"Some power, position and prestige I have," he grexed*, "when I cannot even prevent the Deacons from carrying off my second-eldest-daughter-and-eleventh-child to make her a Temple whore!"

"You have done your best, Papa," chorused Dalassa's several brothers, sisters and tweenies. It was a sentiment with which Dalassa herself thoroughly agreed.

"The quicker I am away," she said soothingly, "the quicker you will be out of trouble with the stone worshippers. My friends here will fly me safely to a snug haven."

"Yes, but *where?*" groaned Borgo Methrix. "All of the Urgovian realms now lie prostrate beneath the iron heel of Soorm; where can you go, and to what snug haven, that their vengeance cannot follow?"

"Actually, I was thinking of Snug Haven," said the imperturbable girl thoughtfully. "You know, on the Isle of Zyle. Or perhaps Safe Harbor. Maybe even Sailors' Rest. . . ."

* A verb peculiar to the syntax of Gondwanish. To *grex* is to grouch, grouse, grumble and gripe, usually in a low, indistinct mutter.

She was listing three small, insignificant seaport towns along the shores of a medium-sized island within the Inland Sea of Zelphodon, of course. One of the Commentaries—I believe it is the Second, but cannot be bothered to look it up now—remarks that the House of the Methrixi had trading connections on Zyle. In fact, a remote cousin and scion of a cadet branch of the House, whose origins were believed to lie in bastardy from the cousin's name, Fitz-Methrix, was resident on Zyle, overlooking the family's mercantile interests in that region.

"First place they'd think of," muttered Borgo gloomily.

"Perhaps, but Soorm has no authority over the Mayoralty of Zyle," Dalassa pointed out.

Her siblings chimed in, the brothers agreeing that Zyle was a good idea, the sisters warning it was too dangerous, and the tweenies, as usual, undecided. Incidentally, Yugg, author of the Twenty-Ninth Commentary, has an interesting note on the tweenies, noted above as the third sex of the Urgovian race. (Yugg the Prurient he was called, since his Commentary deals exclusively with various sexual matters in the epic.) The tweenies, it seems, resemble effeminate boys—or tomboyish girls, as you prefer, but are without the secondary sexual characteristics of either gender. (I cannot, mine being a family publisher, go into any detail as regards their *primary* sexual characteristics.)

Male and female of the Urgovian race, when mated, produce offspring either male, female or tweenie. But when male and tweenie mate, the offspring is always a tweenie. And when female and tweenie mate there is no offspring at all, the union being sterile. A complex system, but not uninteresting: indeed, think how exciting it would be to have *two other entire genders* to be interested in, rather than just one!

"Well, if you must go, then I suppose you had better be off," sighed Borgo Methrix dispiritedly. And he bade his Majordomo to instruct the chef to prepare a large picnic lunch for the travelers, cautioned Dalassa to dress warmly and wear her galoshes in case it rained, pressed gifts on Ganelon and Grrff and even Kurdi, ordered his court jeweler to fabricate posthaste an emerald-studded collar for the Gynosphinx, the gems to be of the exact size and shade of her large green eyes, and went off into his Meditatorium to be alone with his gloomy thoughts.

They departed later on that very day, but, as things eventuated, they did not get very far.

The religion of the Soormians may have been, probably was, a false one. It had been explained to Silvermane that the priesthood had come wandering into these parts of Lower Arzenia about three hundred years ago, and settled among the Stone Heads. The priests were a band of wandering pilgrims, originally devotees of the Hukkite Faith expelled from the cult for nonpayment of dues, briefly turned atheists, then reverting to their former solemn religiosity. They were at that time devotees of no cult in particular, but still they were devotees, devoutly searching for a god or gods to worship.

For better or worse, they had chosen the Stone Heads, seven immense and lonely specimens of crystalloidal intelligence which had existed for geological epochs on the hillside above Soorm, then a modest watering hole for wealthy tourists from Urgoph and the islands of the Zelphodon.

The Heads—formerly nothing more than a minor curiosity, a small local tourist attraction—promptly became their gods, and the new religion was launched on a note of grim fanaticism, with rigid austerities, a grisly inquisitorial arm, and all the humorlessness and stoic disregard for pleasure and comfort which denotes your true zealot.

More recently, strong political ambitions had entered into the dogma of the cult; the Mysteriarch, Ommo the Eleventh, announced it was the Divine Mission of the United Soormian Orthodoxical Church to infiltrate all of the lands about the sea, uniting them into a Sacred Empire. And doubtless it was in his head that Ommo the Eleventh should become First Emperor thereof; such is usually the motivation behind imperial dreams, even among the clergy.

Well, false or not, the Soormians (or the Stone Heads they worshipped) obviously commanded a variety of supernatural powers. For, as our friends soared aloft and circled over the city astride the broad back of the Gynosphinx, they perceived an odd phenomenon.

Above the city, on the heights which overlooked it, rose the many-tiered temple which was the seat of the Soormian Church and the See of its Mysteriarch, Ommo XI.

From an oval orifice in the topmost tier there eddied into the clear, sunny skies of noontide a dribble of peculiar green smoke. In a very short time, the oddly colored vapor increased enormously in volume, until a vast plume of gaseous jade hung over the city.

Through this green vapor they unfortunately flew,

It smelled rather like incense, thought Silvermane.

Then, for a considerable length of time, he thought about nothing at all.

He was vaguely aware that Ishgadara had diverted her flight and, instead of flying off over the glittering waters of the sea, was curiously descending toward the temple area in an ever-tightening spiral. But, although aware of this, he did not seem to be bothered by this to any extent. He glanced around unconcernedly, enjoying the sunny vista of the coast which stretched away to either side, dotted by small farms, laced through with irrigation ditches, traversed by the shining breadth of the Kurge's mouth. Far out on the broad bosom of Zelphodon, small islands were scattered like beads from a broken necklace. Here and there, ships so small as to seem exquisitely crafted miniatures plied the green waters. Seabirds circled, squawking. The air was fresh and bracing, redolent of salt water.

They settled to the top of the tier and were assisted down by stern-faced members of the Proctorial Arm. Smiling bemusedly to themselves, causelessly happy, the travelers permitted themselves to be led away.

And before long they drifted into a deep sleep, still unaware or at least unconcerned over what had so strangely befallen them.

It seemed to Ganelon that, in his dreams, a harsh droning voice was haranguing him about unimportant matters. Indifferently, he listened; he understood what the voice was saying, but was not particularly interested.

The voice was explaining that the Talking Heads were a form of life infinitely superior to True Men, or to anything else on Gondwane, for that matter.

For uncountable and interminable ages they had resided deep within Old Earth; gradually, over immeasurable eons, sentience had dawned within them until they in time had become self-aware. Then a gigantic convulsion of geologic forces had raised them to the planet's surface. The erosion of water, wind and weather had eventually scoured them free of mineral incrustations. Attuning their dormant senses to the vibrations of sound and light, they saw and heard and began to understand and interpret what they now could perceive.

A billion years older than humankind, they would outlive him by a billion years. Not until the moon fell and the sun burned out to a frigid black cinder and Old Earth itself crumbled and decayed into the primal *ylem* from which it had been shaped in the Beginning—then and then only would their consciousness terminate with their existence.

And this might not occur until the final energy death of the universe itself.

Older than men, eternal, fathomlessly wise, unstirred by the hungers and passions of the flesh, they were ineffably superior to all other life forms, and preeminently deserving of the worship of lower life forms.

Their will was not to be questioned, only obeyed. Indeed, considering their omniscience, any opinion which differed from or clashed with their will was a horrendous sin.

Indeed, from the viewpoint of the Heads themselves, any difference of opinion was nigh inconceivable, repellently unnatural, distinctly perverse.

They did not labor for the betterment of man, nor for his perfection: for only they were Perfected. Man existed only to toil for them; it was his blissful purpose in the Scheme of Things to serve the Heads. He had no other purpose in life, and existed solely to serve those superior in every way to himself.

The vapid chauvinism of this inane, pompous lecture began to irritate Ganelon Silvermane, steeped in rosy dreams though he was. He pried open his eyes and looked about for the source of these nonsensical preachments, and found it: a grossly fat, repulsively painted old man squatting on a throne-like platform of solid gold. As he talked in his hoarse, metallic voice, the fat man punctuated his sermon with sweetmeats which he was continuously popping into his thick, wet mouth with greasy fingers.

Before him, kneeling in a semicircle, hands clasped reverently to their breasts, were a bevy of clergymen. Deacons in black, Abbots in yellow, Proctors in red, Oracles in green, Priests in white, and Bishops, Bonzes, Lamas and Shamans in a variety of other hues.

Ganelon wished to scratch his head, found that he could not move his hands, which were behind his back, glanced woozily back over his shoulder, saw that he was tied to an upright post buried in the earth. This annoyed him slightly.

He looked to either side.

Similarly tied to a row of stakes were Dalassa, Grrff, and young Kurdi.

Ishgadara, unfitted by nature to stand comfortably erect, had been wrapped in ropes until she resembled an enormous caterpillar in a cocoon. She lay at the end of the row of stakes, prone on the ground.

His companions were staring with glazed, half-open eyes at the fat man on the dais, still gobbling sweets and sermonizing in his grating tones. They were, apparently, still deep in the drugged trance induced by the green vapor through which they had so unwarily flown.

From the position of the sun, it was early afternoon. They may have been there, tied to the stakes, drinking in that insipid theology for an hour or so, perhaps more.

They were out of doors, Ganelon knew, and he guessed correctly that they were in the Holy Hills. Indeed, lifting his eyes beyond where Ommo squatted, stuffing himself and preaching, he saw the Heads themselves.

They were, it must be admitted, an impressive sight.

Seven in number, the Stone Heads were imbedded in the dead clay of the hill slope. Each was as tall as a man was high, immense boulders of some unknown scarlet mineral, whose surface glinted in the sunlight as if from flakes of mica.

At some period, perhaps before the coming of the Hukkites, they had each been sculpted into the likeness of a man-like visage.

One scowled, one leered, one snarled, one laughed, one howled, one smiled, and one was imperturbably expressionless and serene. Ganelon thought he detected a resemblance to the exaggerated expressions carved on the Heads and the mask of bright red lines that had been tattooed on the faces of the Deacons Ildth and Pervwyn. They were, you will recall, the two Deacons who had captured Dalassa and Kurdi in the Desolation of Oj the previous dawn.

The carven eyes of the Heads were of a stone somewhat different from the rest of their visage. Whereas the scarlet stone of the Heads was rough and porous, resembling coral or even lava, the stone of the eyes had been polished smooth, so that it gleamed like rubious crystal. The ghostly glimmer of a cold, emotionless, utterly alien sentience gleamed discernibly within those stony orbs.

By this point in his interminable harangue, the Mysteriarch

had gotten around to the condemnation. Ganelon began again to pay attention to what the fat man was saying.

He was explaining that, by acting contrary to the express will of the Heads the prisoners were in grave and perilous contravention of the Natural Order of Things. This was not only a sin but a Heresy of the Utmost Degree of Abomination, detested alike by Nature and the Divinities which ruled her.

The girl, already selected for service to the Carnate Ones (and here he ogled Dalassa with a lingering, lascivious gaze), would do penance for her flight by spending ten days in the stocks. The others, however, outlandish foreigners that they were, and doubtless hopelessly lost to the True Faith, were condemned to death by Howling.

At this point, Grrff snorted derisively. He, too, had awakened from the drugged stupor, although a while after Ganelon, and had by now taken everything in. The two warriors exchanged a glance. The expression on the furry face of his friend conveyed to Silvermane as clearly as could spoken words, "Ready when you are, big man."

Dalassa, also awake by now, was looking stubbornly rebellious. She held her chin up and looked bravely at the scowling, leering, snarling, laughing, serene, howling, smiling stone faces. Kurdi and Ishgadara now blinked back to consciousness, looking about them in bewilderment.

Then began the Howling.

Ganelon had earlier inquired of Borgo Methrix if the Heads truly could talk. It seemed that they could, by projecting fields of electromagnetic tension which created a resonance, a vibration, in the molecules of the air.

As for the Howling, it was their way of punishing transgressors. A dull, bone-aching subsonic drone it was, which ascended the scale to an ear-torturing squeal which burst blood vessels in the brain and drove men mad.

Now, as the deep drone began to sound from the air before the Talking Heads, Ommo XI and his followers hastily began stuffing soft wax into their ears.

The Howling rose in timbre, becoming painfully loud.

But Ganelon and Grrff, impatient, began to act. They had by now had enough of this nonsense. Reaching behind them, they grabbed the posts to which each were tied. Huge thews swelled along their shoulders. They *tugged*—

And the Howling became unbearable torment.

5.

DECLINE AND FALL IN SOORM

Ganelon was the first to pull the sharpened end of his stake up out of the ground. With outraged yells, barely audible against the shrill throbbing sound emanating from the Heads, members of the Proctorial Arm of the Church came pelting across the clay soil to arrest him.

Ganelon bent, swivelled lithely to one side. The butt of the heavy stake, swinging through the air like a monstrous bludgeon, caught the first Proctor aside the head and knocked him flying. The second sprawled with a smashed skull. Two others jumped backwards in alarm.

Gritting his teeth, Ganelon burst the ropes which had confined his wrists. Then, seizing up one end of the stake, he charged the priests, employing the long post like a battering ram. They scattered to every side.

Grrff soon had freed himself in like fashion, and the two warriors wreaked bloody ruin among the Proctors, swinging their stakes with devastating effect.

The Howling wobbled, fell, ceased with a squawk of tortured molecules.

"Stop . . . that . ɪ . you . . . humans," said the Scowling Head in slow, heavy, ponderous syllables.

"Yes," agreed the Laugher. "Stop . . . them . . . priests."

Ganelon and Grrff paid no attention to this but proceeded to batter and bludgeon the cultists until no further organized opposition presented itself. Then Ganelon began to clamber up the hillside, his booted feet kicking footholds in the soft, crumbling clay.

"By . . . acting . . . contrary . . . to . . . our . . . will

44

. . . you circumvent . . . the natural . , . order," explained
the Serene Head in calm, reasonable tones. It went on to
patiently point out that the planet is maintained among the
spheres only by its adherence to the natural order, and that
the inquity of their heretical acts was a form of suicidal
cosmic sabotage.

But Ganelon paid no attention to this. Mounting to the top
of that particular Head, he inserted the pointed end of his
stake between the curved stone brow and the spongy clay,
drove it in as deeply as he could, and began to use the stake
as a lever, prying the huge red boulder entirely out of the hill
slope.

Trembling with fury atop his dais, Ommo harshly
commanded his scattering followers to menace the girl and
boy—still safely bound to their stakes—with knives. That, he
reasoned, should end the revolt.

The plodding voice of the Serene Head broke off in a
startled squawk as Ganelon pried it out of the clay. It fell
ponderously—squashing   the   Mysteriarch   flat   in   its
progress—and split apart into several fragments. The glimmer
of sentience within the crystalline eyes ebbed and faded as
they shattered to powder against the edge of the dais.

Grrff, following Silvermane's lead, loosened the Howling
Head. It fell clear—hit the hard ground—cracked—
bounced—and rolled smack into a gaggle of Deacons and
Abbots, flattening most of them.

"How . . . dare . . . you . . . commit . . . such . . . a
. . . sacrilege," pompously (if a bit indistinctly) rumbled the
Leering Head as Ganelon pried it clear. It went off down the
sloping ground, rolling heavily end over end, and dwindled in
the distance. When last seen, it was traveling in the direction
of the town.

"Oh . . . no . . . you . . . don't . . . stop . . .
sombody," muttered the Scowler as Grrff, with a huge grin,
pried it loose. It fell, crushing two Bishops and a young
Acolyte, petrified with fear. It also broke up into many fragments.

Some of the more alert and sensible Proctors, who had
kept their wits about them, had headed off in the direction of
the town. Now they could be seen trotting back from Urgoph, having roused the Civic Guards and a sizable number
of Urgovians converted to the Faith. Ganelon loosened the
Smiler and sent it rolling ponderously like a very juggernaut
down the slope. It came rolling down upon the militia,

smashing several, breaking various arms and legs and heads, scattering the rest of them like tenpins. Nor did it stop there, but rolled on through Urgoph and dropped off the end of a pier into the waters of Zelphodon, still heavily complaining to the last gurgle.

One by one, Ganelon and Grrff dug the Seven Heads out of the clay slope of the Holy Hillside and sent them rolling off. Some struck unsentient boulders and shattered. Others rolled down into the town, breaking apart when they collided with fountains, statues and civic monuments. One swerved, due to a bump in its path which had once been a particularly obese Bishop, and went rolling into the Temple.

Here the gradually sloping decline sharpened, so by the time it reached the Temple precinct it had picked up enough speed to go crashing straight through the outer wall. It vanished from sight, but the adventurers later learned it had ended its travels against the enormous stone column which soared up from the center of the Temple to support the great dome.

The dome shivered, cracked, and collapsed in grandiose slow motion, raining bricks down on the covey of startled Priests, Acolytes, and Abbots who had survived the carnage in the hills and had mistakenly sought refuge within the Temple.

On its travels it had been implored by one singularly devout Bonze, directly in its path, to spare a True Believer.

"Sorry . . . but . . . I . . . can't . . . help . . . myself," it intoned gloomily, as it rolled over the poor Bonze, flattening him on its way through the wall.

And so declined—and fell—the Talking Heads of Soorm. Even if any of their worshippers still retained their Faith and managed to find one of them whose dignity, to say nothing of the rest of his person, was still intact, it is to be doubted if any would bother listening anymore to their solemn pomposities.

Nothing so injures the prestige of a religion as when its gods and idols are toppled from their high places and sent rolling about the countryside like so many sentient but helpless bowling balls.

By this time it was late afternoon, and Ganelon and Grrff the Xombolian had put in a hard day and were rather weary.

They freed Dalassa and Kurdi and Ishgadara from their bonds. Dalassa was so happy and relieved at the splendid way everything had turned out that she impulsively threw her arms around Ganelon's neck and gave him a passionate kiss. He flushed crimson, disentangling himself from the impetuous girl with some difficulty, but as hastily as he could manage it, as she showed every sign of wanting to say thank you several more times in the same manner.

Once they had all greeted one another, and had reassured themselves that all or none of them had sustained any injury from their ordeal, they went searching for their gear and weapons. These they eventually found in the now-deserted and more-than-partly wrecked Temple. The Silver Sword and the Tigerman's ygdraxel and all of their gear, including the Gynosphinx's saddlebags containing the yet-unsampled picnic lunch ordered up for them by Borgo Methrix, they found heaped up in a jumble before the High Altar.

Outfitting themselves again, they left the wrecked Temple and started off down the road toward the town.

"Odd, isn't it?" observed Ganelon Silvermane thoughtfully, a perplexed frown upon his brows, "that nobody has yet come up from town to see what's happened up here."

"It *is*, now that you mention it," said Dalassa, trudging along at his side. (They were walking down to Urgoph because being bound for so long had cramped Ishgadara's wings and she felt a little too lame in the wing joints to fly them there right away.)

"Ol' Grrff w'd of thought, by now, lass, yer father and a deputation from town'd be up here t'congratulate us on overthrowing them priests," muttered the Karjixian, hefting his ygdraxel and looking a bit worried.

"Don't s'pose anything's *happened*, d'ya?" chirped Kurdi brightly.

"What could pe happeningk?" scoffed Ishy cheerfully, waddling along behind her friends.

The hills blocked most of their view of Urgoph from this bend in the dirt road, and all they could spy from here was the occasional red-tiled rooftop and two spires of the Magnatorial Palace.

Still, it *did* seem odd.

As they got closer to the outskirts of the town, the mystery only deepened. You would have thought that, however frightened they may have been earlier to see the dislodged Stone Heads go rolling through the streets, complaining as they fell off into the sea, by now more than a few of the

bolder and more venturesome of the Urgovians would have
come out of the town, at the very least, to see what had eventuated on the hills of Soorm.

But there was nobody at all within the gates. Not even the
Guardsmen who were usually posted there. Everybody
seemed to have congregated toward the southern side of the
town, where the harbor was. And, as the travelers entered the
open, unguarded gates, they saw to their bewilderment that
the squares and streets, bazaars and markets, forums and al-
ley-ways of Urgoph were completely deserted.

Grrff pricked up his ears, sensing a distant din.

"Sounds like they be celebratin' er sumthin'," he grumbled
uneasily.

"Doesn't sound like a celebration to me," commented
Ganelon Silvermane, a bit dubious. "I hear screaming. . . ."

"Maybe it's just *cheering*," said Grrff, although by now
he wasn't too sure.

"Great Gux," gasped the girl, "I think they're *fighting!*"

"Fightin', eh?" rumbled Grrff, hefting his Tigermanic
weapon warily. "Fightin' *who?* We done scattered alla them
priests to here and gone . . . most of 'em ain't gonna slow
down till they reach Runcy."*

"I think you're right, it does sound like fighting," remarked
Silvermane grimly.

And indeed it did! As they traversed the town, the clashing
of swords against shields rang out over a hubbub of men
hoarsely cursing, shouting, yelling, and—more than a few—
screaming as steel bit their vitals.

"I think we'd better hurry along and see what has happened," said Silvermane, unlimbering the Silver Sword and
breaking into a jogging stride. Dalassa, trotting along beside
him was the first to smell smoke. Only a moment or two later
they saw inky black smoke rising from distant houses, which
were evidently in flames.

The adventurers ran across the deserted town, coming
steadily nearer to the noisy scene of battle. Then, rounding a
turn, they came to a huge plaza which faced upon the harbor, and stopped short at the astounding sight which greeted
their eyes.

---

* A small city in Southern YamaYamaLand near the Smoking Mountains. Several thousand leagues from Soorm, it was the most distant
place Grrff could think of on the spur of the moment. That, at any
rate, is the guess hazarded by the author of the Seventeenth Commentary on the Epic.

It was a pitched battle!

The townsmen, hunched down behind hastily improvised barricades built of boxes, bales, barrels, furniture from the nearer of the houses, and anything else they could find, were hurling bricks and bottles.

Some were armed with clubs or rude staves; a few had swords (rusty ones, at that), and some were brandishing spears, javelins or gardening tools. One burly Urgovian was wielding (with considerable effectiveness) a heavy, long-handled bronze maul.

The Civic Guards were, of course, in charge of the Townie side of the conflict. Alas, their functions were essentially ceremonial, and, aside from tossing the local drunk in the clink for disturbing the Civic Peace, they were unused to combat. Theoretically, they were organized to keep the peace and to quell any riots, insurrections, revolts, revolutions, outbreaks of mob violence, looting and general lawlessness as might disrupt the calm of the realm.

In point of fact, however, the Urgovians being a docile and law-abiding lot, none of these things had ever happened, so they had never had to deal with them.

Which placed the poor Guardsmen at a distinct disadvantage, being novices when it came to Being Invaded.

For that seemed to be exactly what was happening here.

Drawn up along the seawall which circled the harbor of Urgoph, four lean, slim, dangerous-looking and decidedly raffish ships stood. Pouring over their sides came a yelling onslaught of dark, dirk-wielding men in swashbuckle boots, bottle-green breeches, silk shirts open to the navel. Scarlet kerchiefs were bound about their brows while gold bangles flashed from their earlobes.

Some were swarthy and black-bearded; others lean, with scarred and wolfish faces and cold eyes.

Quite a few of them held cutlasses between their teeth.

The adventurers stopped short, staring about with astonishment.

"Great Gux, we're being *invaded!*" yelled Dalassa.

"Yeah, an' by *pirates*, too, from th' looka them," growled Grrff zestfully. The battle with the priests had been a minor skirmish as far as the big Karjixian was concerned. He was a warrior . ... and warriors want *war*.

And there looked to be enough war here to satisfy even Grrff the Xombolian! Without further ado, Ganelon and

Grrff plunged into the forefront of the defense, shouldering aside the hunkered-down Urgovians, and taking their stance.

The horde of screeching pirates came pelting across the plaza, waving their dirks, dags, stilettos, cutlasses and scimitars. They were also armed with such typically Gondwanish weapons as the zikko, the pornoi, the sea-trident, the dart-thrower, the sting-sword and the volusk. More than a few held the deadly giz.

And, before you could say "Great Galendil," the battle was joined.

Book Two

PIRATES OF ZELPHODON

The Scene: Aboard the *Bucket o' Blood* on the Sea of Zelphodon; the Isle of Korscio; the Zingaree Atoll.

New Characters: Zarcas the Zirian, Black Horrog, Squint, Patch, and Other Pirates; Zork Aargh, the Vandalexian Mechanoid; Various Islanders; Some Ookaboolaponga Savages.

6.

DEFENDERS ONE, INVADERS NOTHING

The pirate flotilla had landed most of the men in its crews by now, leaving only a skeleton contingent behind to guard against any surprise boarding the villagers might hazard. These worthies lined the rails, observing what they had obviously assumed would be a fray of the short-and-sweet variety. From their negligent posture and the bland or relishing smirks which adorned their greasy or bewhiskered visages, it could be clearly seen that the pirates anticipated only a half-hearted and thoroughly ineffectual resistance from the Urgovians.

They had expected nothing like Ganelon, Grrff or Ishgadara.

Roaring thunderously, nape-fur hackles a-bristle, the Karjixian cleared the crude barricade at a leap which would have done credit to one of his purely feline ancestors. This catlike spring terminated in the very midst of the forefront of the attackers, and Grrff met them lustily, wielding his terrible ygdraxel.

His first opponent, a burly, blue-bearded Julnaritish buccaneer, he neatly disemboweled with a single fluid thrust-and-twist of his claw-bladed weapon. The second he decapitated (de-*faced*, to be accurate), and the third promptly lost his right arm to the shoulder. In no time the Karjixian was surrounded by heaps of the dead and dying, not to mention the dismembered and disabled. Roaring and yowling

53

one of his Tigermanic war songs, Grrff was happily in his element.

Nor was Ganelon Silvermane far behind him. The Silver Sword was a less exotic weapon than the Xombolian's ygdraxel, but no whit less deadly. Its glittering argent metal—hardened by Fire Magic till it was twenty times tougher than steel—clove through bone, brain, brawn and gristle as if meeting no discernible obstacle. And considering the height of Silvermane, the hugeness and breadth of his shoulders, the length of his powerful arms, and the super-human musculature of his physique, the slaughterous efficiency of the sword was only to be expected.

Clearing the barrier with an ease and agility at least comparable to Grrff's, Ganelon took his stance with legs spread, weight balanced on the balls of his feet, and, seizing the two-handed broadsword in precisely the identical grip wherewith a ballplayer seizes his bat, he swung it whistling through the sunny air in a horizontal stroke.

His first pirate, a fat moon-faced Clovian, he cut entirely in two. The fellow had been roaring at the time, and brandishing a cutlass. The upper half of him (still roaring and, in fact, still brandishing) went flying over Silvermane's right shoulder to land with a grisly thump somewhere atop the barricade. The lower half, legs still pumping, waddled clumsily past Silvermane to collide, kicking feebly with rapidly diminishing stride, against the barrier.

The second and the third of the Zelphodonian buccaneers met a comparably swift and gory end. Thereafter the invasion paused, hesitated, and dissolved, forming dual rings about the two champions. But, as their fellows crowded close behind them, the men in front were jostled within reach of the clashing ygdraxel and the whistling Silver Sword. And the dead were heaped at their feet in veritable cartloads.

Nor was Ishgadara idly standing by as a mere observer to the carnage. The sphinx-girl was no warrior, but neither was she lacking in the courage department. She took, in fact, a careless and cavalier attitude towards fighting: she would just as soon not, but, on the whole, what the hell. That about sums up Ishy's philosophy about getting into brawls.

So the Gynosphinx cleared the barricade with a brisk flexing of her wings (still a bit lame and stiff) and hurtled into the yelling mob like a living juggernaut. The several tons of her bowled pirates off their feet by the dozens, and more than a few were crushed under her weight. Then, rearing up on her hind legs, she began playfully flicking out with her paws to right and to left. With each flick, each casual tap or slap, spines snapped, skulls shattered, shoulders crunched gooily.

In all their gore-drenched and criminous careers, the corsairs had yet to encounter a single foe as indomitable as Ganelon or Grrff or the Gynosphinx. And here, in the waterfront marketplace of Urgoph, they faced all three of them. It was enough to make any self-respecting buccaneer reconsider rather seriously his perhaps hasty choice of profession.

While the Construct, the Tigerman and the sphinx-girl held at bay some two hundred pirates—the total was diminishing quite rapidly, at an overall rate of about fourteen every thirty seconds—the two commanders of the raid, from a position of strategic safety in the rear, were wondering what was going wrong. From where they stood, of course, they could see little of the one-sided carnage. But they could hear the deep-chested yowling of Grrff at work, and could glimpse the flying, glittering, metallic mane of Ganelon above the heads of the buccaneers, and could also see the bronze wings and toothy grin of Ishy as she towered above the throng.

Of these dual commanders, the younger and more handsome by far was one Zarcas the Zirian. He was a raffishly good-looking swashbuckler: tall, long-legged, lean and sinewy, with a bronze tanned face in which his white teeth flashed attractively when he smiled. He was not smiling now, was Zarcas; in fact, his clean-shaven, lean-jawed features were screwed up in a bewildered scowl.

His glistening black locks were caught back under a scarlet kerchief, and gold hoops bobbled in the lobes of his ears in the approved, immemorial piratical fashion. His upper torso, impressively muscled and richly tanned, was bare, save for several necklaces of gold chain and precious stones (and a peculiar emerald-green insignia tattooed above his brown left nipple. His long lean legs were clad in bottle-green tights and he wore high seaboots of glistening yellow leather, with high heels and silver buckles on them. A crimson sash was wound about his narrow waist. In one hand he negligently dangled a fencing epée. He had a Past.

His fellow commander was a study in virtually complete contrast. Where Zarcas was clean-shaven and good-looking, Black Horrog was burly, bush-bearded and bearlike, with a broken nose and belligerent, albeit bleary, eyes. He was dark and greasy, his swarthy, pock-marked features scored with thin sallow lines which were scars from many a duel or battle. His thick, tangled red mane and bushy beard were as greasy as his complexion, and his bull-chested body was completely covered with layer on layer of food-stained, wine-spotted finery.

Horrog wore a loose white silk blouse open at the throat to permit his hirsute pelt to be admired by those who admire hirsute pelts. (He was almost entirely covered with hair, doubtless an atavism inherited from his maternal grandmother, who happened to be a Bear.) Over this he wore a scarlet velvet long-coat which had formerly belonged to the late Lord High First Admiral of Otzwotz. It was extremely greasy and bore many stains, some of them blood. He also wore trousers, but they were loose and baggy, and had to be, because of his tail. They were of purple silk, the trousers I mean, and had maroon stripes down their sides. They were tucked into remarkably muddy and beat-up-looking boots whose folded-back tops were usually stuffed with gems and gold coins purloined from the plunder of raped ships and looted villages, in callous defiance of the articles under which he and his crew sailed the high seas of Zelphodon.

He also wore a sash, of golden cloth-of-gold, and over it a much smaller sash of sky-blue silk, and over that a thick and heavy leather girdle (stuffed full of dirks and darts and daggers). These served in part to squinch in his enormous hairy paunch, and also to hold his pants up.

Black Horrog didn't have a past in the sense that Zarcas had a mysterious and romantic one. His past was filled only with hideous tortures, horrendous massacres, horrible treacheries, and like that. The usual sort of thing you would expect of a buccaneer.

Considering his thick, untidy red hair and kinky red beard, it was a little curious that he was called "Black Horrog" instead of "Red Horrog." The fact of the matter was that there had been a very famous (notorious, rather) Zelphodonian pirate called Red Horrog; now retired on Arjis, the pirate stronghold, he was jealous of his reputation. So the younger Horrog had been forced, by the Unwritten Code of the Bloody Brotherhood, to dye his hair and beard or to adopt the apellation of "Black Horrog," although he was really red-haired. He drew the line, however, at dyeing his hair black to match his new name. This was partly because he would have had to dye himself all over . . . A good reason not to, if you think about it.

Zarcas the Zirian was captain of the sloop *Bucket o' Blood*, a craft as lean and dark and rakish as its captain, and which was now drawn up to the pier under the command of his First Mate, Squint.

Black Horrog was captain of the caravel *Black Bessie*, which was as broad in the beam, and every bit as sloppy and disreputable, as its captain. It, too, was drawn up to the pier, and Horrog had left his Second Mate, Zilch, in command. (His First Mate, Hookhand, he had clapped in irons the night before for a fancied slight, something about "hairy Horrog.")

The other two ships in the pirate flotilla were the *Sea Dog* and the *Red Rover*. Their crews had been recruited from the dregs and gutter-sweepings of Orgaza, the Tortuga-like pirate city on Arjis Isle, where the Zelphodonian buccaneers rested and caroused between their sea ventures. They were under the command of Vlasko and Zollobus.

The flotilla, when first organized, had seemed like a good idea. Urgoph was guarded only by its Civic Guard and they were regarded as a cinch. The whole town bulged with warehouses full of loot, and the Magnates were rich with plunder. The port had sounded like a pushover.

But now it was the *pirates* who were being pushed over. This baffled Zarcas as much as it enraged and infuriated Black Horrog. A good plan is a good plan, and nobody likes to see one botched. And this one was, very rapidly and very completely, being botched. Zarcas began to accuse Horrog of being mainly responsible for the botching. And Horrog began to curse and vilify Zarcas on the same point.

"If you'd agreed with my plan to attack at night, under cover of darkness, you hairy hulking horror, we'd of had no trouble," said the Zirian sharply.

"Izzat so, ya spindle-shanked galoot," growled Horrog, baring his yellowed fangs and tusks.* "An' if you'd'a lemme bombard th' town wif Heek Fire, like I wanted ta, we'd'a had

---

* This is not merely auctorial exaggeration, I will have you know. Black Horrog really *did* have fangs and tusks, not being a True Man as Zarcas was. He had a tail, too, although few of his fellows had ever seen it—Horrog never bathed and could not swim, and doesn't seem to have taken his clothes off very often. The Twelfth Commentary assures us of these facts, and who am I to dispute the sagacious Ivvriel?

'em all hidin' ina hills afore we landed! An' who you callin' a hairy hulkin' horra, ya girl-faced ginch?"

The accusational exchange had by this point become not only extraneous but verged on peril. This was because by now the entire attacking force was in full flight, and looked about to trample its two organizers underfoot at any moment. Black Horrog took refuge under a convenient barrel and Zarcas took to his heels, sprinting back to the *Bucket o' Blood* just before the first of his panicky crew got there.

(Incidentally, Heek Fire was very much the same as the ancient "Greek Fire"—a combustible fluid launched from ballistae in frangible ceramic containers—except that, in this case, it was invented by the Heeks. The Heeks were an extinct maritime civilization which flourished about the isles and archipelagoes of the Zelphodon in former epochs, and reinvented the lost arts of naval warfare.)

Within moments the stampeding buccaneers were piling aboard their vessels, scrambling and scrabbling to get beyond the reach of the three defenders. Some of them leaped from the piers and splashed and gargled to their ships, shinnying up the rigging or the anchor cables. Others galloped up the gangplanks. A few climbed the figureheads. Before long, the whole mob of them were aboard their crafts, which were weighing anchor and putting back out to sea again.

Grrff had enjoyed the battle so much that he was reluctant to see it end. So he followed, chasing the fleeing pirates as they took to their heels. In his very commendable zeal to punish the malefactors, however, the Tigerman went charging up the gangplank of the *Bucket o' Blood*, and waded into the crowd which thronged the deck, and began plying his ygdraxel, as was his wont.

Ganelon, seeing Grrff bounding along after the pirates, ran to join him; and, in fact, so did Ishgadara. Clinging to her shoulders, Ishy had two passengers, for little Kurdi and that bold bonde girl, Dalassa, had climbed upon her broad back and had been wielding swords snatched up from the ground. Dalassa was, it seems, somewhat braver and more outspoken than most of her fellow Urgovians. Between them, the gypsy boy and the beautiful golden-haired girl had accounted for a modest share of the piratical dead.

By the time the ships had put out to sea again, the Civic Guard broke ranks and flocked to the ends of the piers, waving farming implements and calling the pirates rude names.

They were terrible fighters, those Urgovians—once the battle had been won for them by someone else, that is.

Ganelon and his companions did not at first realize their predicament. Then, as the pirates backed away, leaving them alone on deck, ducking down into the holds and through trapdoors and so on, the Tigerman began to notice something.

For one thing, there was no longer anyone to kill.

For another, the deck was rocking slowly underfoot.

Exactly like a ship at sea.

He glanced back at the rapidly receding shoreline, and realized gloomily that the ship *was* at sea.

"Oh-oh," said Grrff unhappily.

He tore the clothing off the nearest corpse and moodily cleaned the reeking gore off the hook-blades of his ygdraxel.

Ganelon, Ishgadara, Kurdi and Dalassa had by now realized that they had been just a trifle rash in following the pirates on board the *Bucket o' Blood*.

This was brought home to them rather forcibly when suddenly a row of kerchiefed grinning heads popped up over the rail of the afterdeck. The heads had arms and hands attached to them in the usual manner. These hands, however, were holding bows and arrows, and there was something in the way they handled them that suggested a thorough and deadly competence with their employment.

Zarcas now came strolling up to the little group who had so gallantly defended Urgoph. Smiling, suave, debonair and unruffled, he made a courtly bow, sweeping the gore-splattered deck with the plumes of his wide-brimmed hat. The plumes were crimson, anyway, so it didn't much matter if he got a little blood on them.

"Gentlemen—and ladies," he said with a flashing smile, "if I may make so bold as to introduce myself, I am Captain Zarcas of the Bloody Brotherhood—at your service!"

Ganelon stolidly introduced himself and the others. To each, the Zirian buccaneer made a small, mocking bow.

"As owner and chief officer of your present conveyance," he grinned wickedly, "may I invite you to make yourself at home aboard the good ship *Bucket o' Blood*. It will, in fact, be your home for the next several weeks."

"Izzat so?" growled Grrff truculently.

"It is indeed so, my furry friend," said Zarcas. "The archers on the afterdeck will, perhaps, not have escaped your keen and catlike eye. I am well aware that this winged lady

can fly: or at least, I strongly suspect that her alate append-
ages are not dysfunctional and purely ornamental. But no one
can fly when he, she or it is riddled through and through with
arrows."

A glum silence was the only answer he received to this ob-
servation. Across the green waters of the Zelphodon, the
brightly colored roofs of Urgoph receded in the distance. The
scarlet sails of the black sloop boomed in the wind like
drums. The salty breeze hummed and sang in the rigging.

"Now shall we discuss the terms of your surrender?" suggested Zarcas the Zirian politely.

7.

ZARCAS THE ZIRIAN

During the next two weeks, Ganelon Silvermane and his companions became accustomed to living aboard a ship.

The experience was a novelty for all of them, with the single exception of Dalassa the Urgovian girl, who had been in and out of boats all her life.

But the others were born or raised far inland, and had never before been at sea. In fact, the largest body of water any of them had enjoyed prior experience with was the Greater Pommernarian Sea, which was the site of the Mad Empire of Trancore. Or, perhaps, the broad expanse of Lake Xor near the northerly borders of Greater Zuavia, where the island city of Pathon Thad is. (I am uncertain which of the two is the larger; anyway, they were both only lakes—this was a real *sea*.)

So the landlubbers had to become accustomed to living on something that pitched and tossed and rolled underfoot with every wave. All of them, except Ganelon, Ishy and Dalassa, lost their lunch a few times, and wished heartily for the arrival of Merciful Death. But seasickness is a disease rarely fatal, and in time all of them got their sea legs, and, if I may say so without vulgarity, their sea stomachs, too.

As to why Zarcas had insisted on their surrender rather than killing them outright, when he so obviously had the chance to do so, the answer is simple. Those who ply his buccaneering trade do so for monetary profit, not pleasure or sport. And there is no profit to be gained from idle or indiscriminate killings.

Among the pirates of the Bloody Brotherhood, Zarcas was

considered quite a comer. His rise through the ranks had been little short of spectacular. Soon, if all went well, he would stand among the greatest and most formidable of the Captains of the Coast. The looting of Urgoph would have been a feather in his cap; since the raid had turned into a debacle of major proportions, he was eager—nay, anxious—to salvage something from what might otherwise go down in the Red Annals of the Brotherhood as "Zarcas' Fiasco."

The damage to his reputation and prestige had been considerable. But . . . to have captured alive the valiant trio of Urgovian defenders who had single-handedly put the pirate horde to rout was, at least, something. And it was not beyond the realm of possibility that the Grand Magnate of Urgoph might pay dearly to ransom his champions,

Anyway, it was worth a try.

They were not mistreated; quite the contrary, in fact. Zarcas proved a generous conqueror, and a gallant host. His urbane wit delighted those of them able to appreciate it—which is to say, Dalassa, mostly. His table groaned beneath rare viands, and his cellar was princely. Moreover, he found in this mixed bag of prisoners objects of considerable curiosity. The brawny frame of Silvermane excited his admiration, as did the warlike prowess and brute courage of Grrff. Kurdi he found amusing and likable; Ishgadara was sheerly fabulous and he enjoyed conversing with her.

And, as for Dalassa. . . .

For their own part, the captives entertained considerable curiosity concerning the antecedents of their host.

"He is a gentleman, I'm sure of it," insisted Dalassa stubbornly. "Of lordly, or at least noble, birth."

"He's a bloody-handed rogue an' reaver," growled Grrff disparagingly.

"He is not!" stated Dalassa, stamping her little foot. "He has treated us with every courtesy—why, we even dine in his cabin every night, like paying guests rather than prisoners! He is a gentleman, fallen on evil times, forced into his gory trade by circumstances beyond his control . . ₁ perhaps, as a babe, he was carried off by wicked sailors . . ."

Grrff grimaced, and spat sourly—out the porthole, I am glad to report.

"He's a pirate," said the Tigerman. "Same thing as bein' a thief; prob'ly a murderer, too."

"He," said Dalassa through clenched teeth, "is of gentle birth and breeding."

Grrff opened his mouth to make some rejoinder or other, but a small sound from behind them caused him to forget what he was going to say. It was a polite clearing of the throat.

They turned: their captainly captor stood in the doorway, impeccably clad in butternut satin, gilt lace frothing at throat and wrists, an emerald as big as a walnut shimmering on the middle finger of one lean brown hand. Captain Zarcas smiled suavely.

"You are both perfectly accurate in your estimates of my humble person," he said imperturbedly. "I am, quite true, of princely birth. Equally true, I follow the piratical trade and am, by definition, both a thief and a murderer. I am also—" (He ticked the ensuing points off on his fingers.) "—An exile from my native land; a condemned criminal; a gentleman of the highest birth and breeding; a convicted traitor to my homeland and under sentence of death; a connoisseur of fine wines, precious gems, good books and beautiful women."

This last was said with a wicked glint in his eye, and a slight, mocking bow in the direction of Dalassa. The blonde girl blushed—and, as she was modestly attired in the fashions of Urgoph, which is to say three small pieces of golden filigree held by silk cords—the blush was clearly observable over a very considerable portion of her lushly curvaceous anatomy. Zarcas and Grrff watched the progress of that blush with awe and masculine interest.

Silvermane had given his word not to attempt an escape, and perforce did not. Grrff, Kurdi and Ishgadara could see no sense in this refusal, and grew (respectively) sullen, curious, and morose. Only Dalassa understood a warrior's honor; for her part, she was surprised that the Karjixian Tigerman did not understand the Heroic Code. When she voiced her surprise on this facet of his character, the furry fellow snorted, wrinkling up his snout.

"Ol' Grrff keeps his word to his friends, sure," he informed the blonde girl. "But not to his enemies. All's fair in love an' war, like we say back home . . . and a good kick in th' pants when a foe's back is turned is okay in our book, too!"

Ganelon, however, would hear nothing of escape. While aboard the *Bucket o' Blood* he would make no attempt at escape; neither would he permit his comrades to attempt it without him. That had been the precise wording of the promise he had made to Captain Zarcas, and he firmly' intended to observe every last syllable of it.

But nothing more. The very moment they landed—at wherever it was they were going—it was his plan to pile his friends aboard Ishgadara's broad and furry back and fly back to Urgoph to deliver Dalassa to her father, the Grand Magnate.

This plan, however, he had not discussed with his fellow captives. The partitions were thin aboard the good ship *Bucket o' Blood,* and the pirates of Zelphodon had ears as sharp as their fingers were sticky. When the time was ripe, he would somehow contrive to pass the word around.

The Zelphodon was broad and green (not blue). This—its greenness, I mean—was due to the fact that, unlike the blue seawater of our own time, it contained no azurium, but plenty of vertium. These common but exceedingly minute and elusive elements had not been discovered in our time. Indeed, it was not until the Eon of the Thought Magicians that the savant Torasco managed to extricate and isolate them.

Azurium happens to be the trace element which gives the color commonly called "blue" to anything, and it is present in enormous quantities in the sea and the sky, blue eyes, blue denims, blueberries, and anything else that is blue. Vertium, it follows, is the trace element which is the source of the color green. It is profusely present in lettuce, grass, emeralds, leaves, certain kinds of jade, spinach, green beans, and so on, not to mention pea soup.

The Zelphodon contained, as said before, no azurium, but lots and lots of vertium. Hence it was green.*

It was also rather enormously large. In our own time, the very largest inland body of water in the world is the Caspian Sea, some one hundred and sixty-nine thousand square miles in extent. Well, sir, the Zelphodon weighed in at one hundred

---

* Azurium is Number 114 on the Periodic Table of the Elements, and has an atomic weight of 264; its discovery was Torasco's first triumph. Vertium, his next discovery, is Element 115, with an atomic weight of 266. He anticipated the subsequent discovery of either purpurium or gulesium, the significant trace elements in everything colored either purple or red, but, unfortunately, succumbed to a surfeit of Unicorn's liver, devoured during a feast held to celebrate his discoveries, and died at table. None of his disciples felt inclined to continue his pioneering work, and it soon languished.

and eighty-three thousand square miles of vertium-rich water. And that is a lot of water, you will agree. Enough to hold three hundred and sixty-seven islands, reefs, archipelagoes and atolls, comprising thirty-eight kingdoms, federations, democracies, empires and anarchates which flourish (more or less) on these intramaritime protuberances. And upon their wealth and produce the Bloody Brotherhood preys.

But there is enough to go around, surely. Take the Kakkawakka Islands, for instance. The savages who inhabit those islands gather pearls, spice, pepper, copra, tea, zonka beans, edible ooky-ooky fruit, the plumes of flying serpents, and Behemoth ambergris.

Or the Isle of Korscio (toward which at this time the pirate flotilla was headed); the Korscioians harvest sea flowers, timber, and gather odorous gums, lapis lazuli, the milk of giant albino spiders (which, when processed, turns into xaxary), and rubies. The yellow kind only.

Or the Zingaree atoll, which was the next stop on the corsairs' schedule. There the natives gather coconuts, coffee beans, several kinds of tasty fish, the horns of sea-unicorns, platinum nuggets washed ashore, and narunga.

Nobody goes hungry.

Ganelon wondered why Zarcas was sailing deep into the Zelphodon, rather than lying offshore and negotiating their ransom with Dalassa's father, the Grand Magnate Borgo Methrix. Since the ransom, which would at least in part mitigate the failure of the expedition against Urgoph, to have lurked near the seaport while exchanging embassies and arguing price and terms, would have seemed the obvious course for the pirate to take. Not so, apparently.

Finally, he asked Squint about it.

Squint, who served his captain in the capacity of First Mate, was a tall, skinny, lemon-yellow Ikzikian with a pointed nose and three ears. He also—obviously—had a bad case of squinting. The fact that Ganelon had never before encountered an Ikzikian during his travels was not surprising, since the race was largely rendered extinct long before his era by an attack of the Giggling Sickness.

Nor did Squint's ears bother him especially. Ganelon was used to encountering strange races by now—like the Voygych River Brigands he had fought back in Malme River Country about a year ago. They had lacked noses, he recalled, and after you have seen men suffering from a lack of noses, extra ears are nothing much.

The funny thing was that Squint could hear as well as anyone. That was because of his very large front teeth, which vibrated to the impact of sound, the impulses communicated to the hearing center of the brain by nerve channels peculiar to the Ikzikian race. Ears had nothing to do with it.

"Capting by goin' to Korscio now on accounta 'tis xaxary season," explained Squint in reply to Silvermane's query. And he expanded on this by going into more detail about the giant albino spiders.

"Tame critters they be," affirmed Squint. "Them Korscioians do herd um. This be milkin' season, y'know, and hit won't be long afore they milk ferments inta xaxary. On'y happings onct a year₁ . . ."

Xaxary is an odorous purple cheese, much prized as a delicacy by the inhabitants of the Zelphodon. Ganelon had never tasted it, and, on the whole, thought he would rather not.

Cheese is cheese, of course. But—cheese from *spiders?*

Squint was not the only member of Zarcas' crew who was not a True Man. Perhaps I should remind my reader here that by the Eon of the Falling Moon the human race was in a distinct minority. As the march of evolution had never faltered or failed, new forms of sentient life had been continuously developing for many millions of years. Grrff's race, the Tigermen of Karjixia, were an example of this—although in their case they had been helped along by a powerful magician, Ganelon's absent-minded friend, the Immortal Palensus Choy. And, I suppose, the Red Amazons, the Death Dwarves, the Mandragons and the Talking Heads of Soorm were other examples. Many in Zarcas' crew were not True Men.

One-Eye, for one. He was enormously huge and heavy, and quite deserved his name. For it was not that he had lost an eye in a fight or an accident, but that he was a Neocyclopian from Quorp and truly had only one eye—bright red, and smack in the center of his forehead.

Then there was Uxab, whose fellow pirates called him Claw. He deserved this appellation since, instead of ordinary hands, his arms ended in two immense yellow pincers for all the world like those of an immense canary-yellow lobster. Claw's lobsterian appearance was further enhanced by his stalked eyes, clashing mandibles, and chitinous exoskeleton of glistening yellow horny stuff. He was in fact the descendant of a race of intelligent crustaceans who generally inhabited the floor of the Sea of Zelphodon, but were true amphibians; Uxab was a trifle more adventurous than the rest of his sedentary, stay-at-home, stick-in-the-mud kind.

Or, for that matter, consider Patch, who shared a cabin with One-Eye and Claw. Like the Neocyclopian, Patch also had only one optic, but in his case the other had been scratched out in a duel and he kept the empty socket politely hidden behind a patch of green yux leather.

Patch's peculiarity was that he was quite transparent. His flesh was glassy and lucent, and you could look through his body and see his various parts and organs gurgling and squishing away inside, busily palpitating or secreting or digesting, or whatever. A walking lesson in anatomy was Patch. He was a former Glunganunga Islander, and the inhabitants of those isles customarily fed on a species of edible (in fact, very tasty) jellyfish. Some generations back, famine had struck the isles, wiping out the rice crop and killing off the tree-dwelling oysters, both of which had served to vary the typical Glunganungan's diet. Settling for jellyfish, the Islanders found that after generations of this dietetic monotony they were gradually becoming as transparent as their staple food. By this time, the race was as transparent as glass.

They didn't much mind; it gave them something to talk about.

The most singular of all the crewmen aboard the good ship *Bucket o' Blood*, however, was not enlisted until the events described in the next chapter.

8.

CURIOUS CUSTOM OF KORSCIO

Exactly two weeks to the day since they had sailed from the harbor of Urgoph the pirate flotilla hove to off the shores of Korscio. The green and palmy isle loomed before them across the sparkling waves.

The night before, Zarcas had summoned the captains of the other ships in the little fleet. They had come rowing in longboats to clamber up the sides of the flagship, where Zarcas entertained them at dinner in his cabin. The commanders of the two smaller vessels had glanced curiously at Silvermane and Grrff and their companions as they came aboard, but paid them little attention. Black Horrog, however, was something else.

The furry buccaneer stopped short at the sight of the prisoners, who were then enjoying a last turn on deck before sitting down to dinner. His bearded visage crimsoning, the pirate chief uttered a strangled oath, giving each of them a baleful glare, before stomping off to join the others in Zarcas' cabin.

"Wonder what's eating him?" rumbled Grrff thoughtfully.

"He certainly didn't look very friendly," remarked Dalassa.

"Ol' Grrff's got a feelin' we're gonna have trouble from *that* direction," said the Tigerman. Later that night, after his visitors had all returned to their own ships, Zarcas made explanation.

"If you can possibly arrange it," suggested the handsome corsair, "I would advise all of you to try and stay out of Captain Horrog's way."

"Why is that, Captain?" asked Ganelon Silvermane.

Zarcas grinned mischievously. "He bears a grudge against you which is perhaps understandable, since it was his crewmen whom you decimated in your admirable and quite successful defense of Urgoph town."

"*His* men?" asked little Kurdi. "Howcum?"

"Well, young 'un, Horrog is the greediest of all the Captains in the Bloody Brotherhood," chuckled Zarcas with a twinkle in his eyes. "When we landed, Horrog's boys crowded into the forefront by shouldering everyone else out of the way. That way, you see, they could make sure of grabbing the lion's share of the plunder and the women. As things turned out, all they got was the lion's share of your glittering steel! At any rate, Horrog has it in for you. So watch your step around him: I want to deliver you hale and whole back to Urgoph, and not in little pieces."

"Well, are we likely to encounter the fellow, Captain Zarcas?" inquired Dalassa pertly. He shrugged.

"Here on my ship, of course, you are safe. But once we return to our home port of Orgaza, on Arjis Isle, you may well run into him—or he into you."

"You are, then, planning to return to the corsair stronghold before communicating your ransom terms to my father in Urgoph?"

"I am. Unfortunately, our schedule demands it. And from Arjis I can communicate well enough with Urgoph by means of seamail."

"Of, of course," she nodded unconcernedly.

This reference to seamail eluded Ganelon Silvermane, who made a mental note to find out later from the blonde girl what it meant.

The attack commenced two hours past sunrise. The pirates drew up to shore and clambered over the side, plopping down into the wet sand of the beach to waddle ashore, clumsy in their seaboots, waving their cutlasses and yelling bloodthirsty threats. Dalassa shuddered, feeling sorry for the poor Korscioians.

Their villages—mere collections of palm-leaf huts between the beach and the jungle's edge, seemed deserted, however. And bales and baskets of goods had been left out. Upon these the buccaneers fell, with loud expressions of glee. The villagers' curious behavior in not defending their goods mystified Silvermane.

"Is it always as easy as this to raid Korscio?" he inquired

of Squint. Squint, who had been left behind with a skeleton crew as usual, sniggered and spat over the side.

"Always," grunted the lanky yellow-skin. "Hit's in our contract."

" *'Contract?'* " demanded Grrff, blinking in incredulity. "You guys gotta *contract* wif the Korscioians t' raid 'em?"

"Yep," said the laconic Squint. Then he chuckled, and gave a toothy leer. "Keep watchin' an' yew'll see hit all."

The prisoners lined the rail, curiously observing the goings-on.

First the buccaneers grabbed up the bags, bales and boxes of loot and plunder, which they lugged down the beach, piled up, and divided between the crewmen of the several ships. The goods—including fat red ceramic jars containing the fragrant spider cheese called xaxary—were hauled aboard the waiting pirate ships in nets swung over the side and lowered into the hold by winches. This was rather quickly accomplished.

Then the pirates went clumping back up the shore to the village, pried off their boots, loosened their neckerchiefs and sashes, and began to eat and drink from the village foodstuffs. Whatever it was they were drinking, it was potent stuff, for in no time they became roaring drunk.

"Don't you envy your comrades their debauch?" inquired Dalassa curiously of Squint. He snorted derisively.

"Not me, missy! Don't be likin' me wimmen fat . . . nemine' . . . keep watchin' . . . yew'll see hit all."

Captain Zarcas had come back aboard by this point in the raid and descended into the hold with Squint to store and log the plunder.

"Look!" squealed Kurdi excitedly.

The first villagers had appeared, stealing timidly from behind the bushes. Ganelon and Grrff looked, and gaped in amazement.

They were all *women*: green of skin as unripe apples, and enormously fat. Their frizzy hair was dyed bright pink. They were also unclothed, except that they wore two red blossoms about the size of hibiscus flowers hung about their middles on single strands of palm fiber. One such blossom dangled fore, the other aft. Neither did very much to veil the dubious charms of the green ladies.

Ogling the boozy pirates, they coyly cooed and giggled, wiggling their remarkable haunches flirtatiously. Not a one of them but would have tipped the scales at three hundred pounds. And now, as reeling pirates paired off with willing—albeit rather hefty—wenches, it became obvious to the watchers why the pirates had gotten so thoroughly drunk before the commencement of the orgy.

"Great Galendil," muttered Grrff faintly, "I'd hafta be soused, too, t' take one a them behind the bushes! Female that size c'ud break a feller's *back*."

Zarcas chuckled from behind them, and they made room for him at the rail.

"Perhaps you could explain?" invited Silvermane, still bewildered.

"Certainly," smiled the corsair. "The Korscioian savages, as you see, live like Amazons, eschewing the companionship of men. For their race to continue into the next generation, however, some form of masculine cooperation is required. The Bloody Brotherhood discovered the lay of the land (pardon the pun, m'lady, it was not intentional) many years ago, and worked out an agreement with the Big Chieftainess of the savages. In return for half their xaxary and a third of the rest of their harvest, the men of the Brotherhood agreed to, ah, 'service' the Korscioians on an annual basis. The raid is due in xaxary-ripening season, that is to say, right now: which is why we had to come to Korscio first, rather than linger off Urgoph to discuss your ransom."

There was a lot of noisy, rhythmic thrashing in the bushes by now, into which the pirates and the fat green ladies had all vanished. Squeals and giggles also could be heard. Dalassa turned away, finding the scene repulsive.

"Come with me, Kurdi, you are too young to observe such barbarity," she said, leading the reluctant lad below decks. Zarcas laughed: Kurdi had been watching the goings-on with slack-jawed fascination.

"So instead of raiding 'em, yer actually *tradin'* wif 'em, eh, Cap'n Zarc'?" rumbled Grrff, winking.

"That's about the size of it," shrugged the Zirian. Then, more tolerantly, "Besides, the boys need a bit of shore leave once in a while . . . and the ladies of Korscio are *most* accommodating."

"How long does this go on?" inquired Silvermane.

"Not long; they'll all be worn out by noontime, I'll warrant."

They lunched on deck and sampled the xaxary cheese, which was indescribably delicious, the flavor being somewhere between sour dungo rinds and overripe yagla sauce, but with a crumbly, sponge-like consistency. Even Ganelon tried it, despite his previous squeamishness, and found it sharp, pungent, and savory.

During the early afternoon, the pirates came ambling out of the jungle, rather shaky in the legs and hung over to a considerable degree. Some of them were so wobbly they had to be helped aboard by their shipmates. All of them fell into their hammocks, bunks or mats and fell asleep instantly, snoring like so many buzzsaws.

"Will we stay here overnight, Captain?" asked Dalassa, back on deck now that the amorous obligations of the Bloody Brotherhood had been paid.

"Usually we do; none of my men exactly feel like hitting the high seas again—at least not right now," he replied.

"What *was* that stuff they was drinkin', anyway?" inquired Grrff.

"Fermented slime of sea snake," said Zarcas succinctly.

"Oog," remarked Grrff, looking a trifle ill. The more he thought about it, the sicker he looked. He would probably have turned green if he hadn't been covered with tiger-striped fur. In fact, beneath the fur he probably did.

"*Ulp.* Don' feel much like hittin' the high seas meself," admitted Grrff to Dalassa. She had a peculiar gleam in her eyes, he noticed. Then, waiting until the Captain went off to his cabin to count pearls or whatever it is that pirate chiefs *do* in their cabin, she spoke to him in an urgent whisper.

"This is our chance, Grrff!"

"Hanh?"

"Our chance to escape, you big lump!"

"Whatcha mean? Big man, he gave his *word*—"

The blonde girl shook her head impatiently. "That was good only aboard the *Bucket o' Blood*, on the high seas! Once we are on land, the agreement is null and void. Don't you remember the terms?"

"Guesso," the Tigerman grunted, looking dubious. Then, he pointed out gently, as if she had somehow managed to overlook the self-evident fact, "We're still on board *ship*, y'know. . . ."

"I know that, you furry idiot," the girl stormed. "But the *ship* is on the *shore*—look over there—see the anchor cable tied to that big rock, right? We're not on the high seas right now. So—technically—we are at liberty to effect our escape. Where's Ishgadara?"

"Over there ahint th' mast, playin' mumbledy-peg wif Squint," he muttered. "But I dunno, gal ₂ . . big man, he's a real stickler fer doin' whut's right . . . dunno whether er not he'll agree we're free t' git away . . ."

"Oh, very well, then," snapped the Urgovian girl. "Then we'll all go for a stroll on the beach; even Ganelon Silvermane will then have to admit we are no longer on the ship and no longer bound by the surrender terms. . . ."

"Think they'll let us?" Grrff murmured dubiously.

Dalassa looked demure.

"I think Captain Zarcas will allow us to stretch our legs on shore a bit—if *I* ask him," she said off-handedly.

The huge Tigerman uttered a sort of strangled, growling snort—his way of chortling. Then he winked ponderously.

"Guess he will, at that," said Grrff humorously. "Cap'n Zarc' is kinda sweet on you, ain't he?"

The girl crimsoned, looking furious. Then she grinned and punched him in the biceps₂

"Get down below, you furry oaf, and pack your ygdraxel and the Silver Sword in Ishgadara's saddlebags. I'll meet you on shore after I've spoken to the Captain. I'll toss the bags over the side so they'll float to shore. With luck, nobody'll see them . . . scoot, now, before something goes wrong!"

With an admiring look after her, Grrff chuckled, and scooted.

Well, Dalassa's plan worked as smoothly as smooth. Whatever blandishments or wiles she employed on Zarcas the Zirian, he agreed willingly enough to her request. After two weeks aboard the cramped little sloop, it was only natural that his involuntary passengers might wish to stretch their legs on dry land with a bit of a stroll.

Bedazzled by the blonde girl's beauty or no, it did not seem to occur to the pirate chief that their passage aboard the good ship *Bucket o' Blood* was, in fact, involuntary.

They clambered over the side, Grrff catching Dalassa in his strong arms, while Kurdi swarmed giggling down the anchor-line.

Ishgadara merely spread her bronze wings with a snap, like a Chinaman whipping open his stiff fan, and soared over the rail to the wet beach. Then—having been tipped off by Dalassa—she waddled on her bowlegs around the prow to salvage the saddlebags from the surf. These she carried in her blunt tusk-like teeth, and, as her back was turned to from the ship, it is to be doubted whether anyone aboard saw or noticed that the sphinx girl was carrying anything.

Ganelon stretched his great arms happily, striding up the curve of the beach, following Dalassa. (She had decided it would be more polite to make their aerial escape from the pirates around the bend, where no one could see them fly away.) The silver-haired giant thought it felt good to stand on dry land again.

No one, of course, had mentioned escape to Silvermane, lest he balk at the plan. The simple, honest Silvermane had, perhaps, an over-developed sense of personal honor.

They vanished one by one around the curve of the beach until they were hidden from the view of the buccaneers behind the palms.

It didn't matter, because no one was watching them, anyway. Most of the pirates were still sound asleep, sunk in slumber, still sleeping off their drunken debauch.

A long moment passed.

Then, suddenly, and also shrilly, Dalassa—*screamed*.

As her terrified shriek knifed through the hot, drowsy afternoon, Zarcas sprang up from his table—he had, as it turned out, actually been counting pearls!—with a curse, suddenly paling to the lips.

Whether or not he was as "sweet" on Dalassa as Grrff had averred, he certainly did seem alarmed at the thought of the blonde girl being in danger.

Clearing the stairs at a bound, maybe *two* bounds, he gained the deck with his swordblade naked in his lean brown hand. Going to the rail he stopped short. And stared open-mouthed.

Rudely jarred from their boozy snorings by Dalassa's screech, the pirates came boiling on deck in various stages of undress, pouring forth for all the world like angry hornets from a nest which someone, most unwisely, has just whacked with a big stick.

They lined the rail. And stopped. And also stared.

Back around the bend of the beach came the would-be runaways, Dalassa sprinting along in the lead, then Kurdi, with Grrff and Ganelon and Ishgadara gallumphing along in the rear. Escape or no escape, they headed for the relative safety of the pirate ship.

And the reason for this untimely reversal of plan would

have been quite obvious to you, could you have seen the ungainly, the fantastic, the astonishing monstrosity of living metal which was clanking along after them as fast as its jointed metal limbs could clank—

9.

ZORK AARGH COMES ABOARD

As you might well expect, our heroes wasted little or no time in getting back aboard the *Bucket o' Blood*. Ganelon Silvermane and Grrff the Xombolian were perfectly willing to do battle against men, mutations and monsters; however, any self-respecting warrior would draw the line at machines.

Grrff swarmed over the side, swearing, hackles abristle, eyes wild. "Git goin'," he said tersely to Squint.

"D'yez be after meanin' 'weigh anchor?'" inquired the yellow skinned Ikzikian.

"Whatever ya call it, *do* it," advised Grrff, starting to climb the mast.

"Here hit comes now, Cap'n," said One-Eye in his heavy voice. The hulking Neocyclops from Quorp hefted a belaying pin dubiously, then tossed it aside and decided to go down in the hold for awhile.

"What is toward?" demanded Zarcas, a mite querulously of Dalassa as he helped her over the rail. "What is that walking tin thing? And where did you find it?"

"Beats me," said Dalassa briefly, in answer to the first query. "And we didn't: *it* found us." She squirmed past Zarcas and went to hide in the hold with One-Eye.

"Be hit *alive*, missy?" whispered Patch to the blonde girl as she went by.

"Alive enough," she remarked, shuddering. "It . . . *spoke* to us!"

"My liver an' lights!" swore Patch feebly. Through his lucent flesh it could clearly be seen that, at the moment, his liver and lights were palpitating with extreme agitation.

Dalassa vanished down the hold, and began arguing with One-Eye about the best place to hide. Ganelon tossed little Kurdi up over the rail, sprang, caught the rail, heaved himself up and over, and gave Zarcas a somber look.

"Better get your ship out of here," he remarked gloomily. "It may try to come aboard."

"Dint yew try t' fight hit, big feller?" croaked Claw, clashing his lobster-like pincers suggestively.

"No," said Silvermane. The obvious absurdity of trying to kill something that wasn't really alive in the first place simply had not occurred to him. And, besides, wouldn't it be futile to go whanging away with your sword against something also made of metal?

"Get ready, men; here it comes," snapped Zarcas, taking his stand beside Silvermane. "Men?" he repeated, turning to glance over his shoulder. Every member of the crew had, however, vanished. Zarcas smiled crookedly. "Some crew *I've* got," he muttered. "Well, then . . . it's you and I alone against the metal monster, my stalwart friend!"

Ganelon glanced around, spotting Grrff in the crow's nest.

"Get down here, Grrff," he commanded sternly.

"Do I gotta?"

"It is imperative."

"Oh, my claws and whiskers!" grumbled Grrff, wishing he had been a coward rather than a warrior. But he began to clamber down the mast, digging his tigerlike claws into the seasoned wood.

An endless moment passed during which nothing at all happened. A flying snake went flapping by, hissing mournfully. A bluebottle buzzed noisily about a puddle of spilt tar. A drop of perspiration trickled down Captain Zarcas' handsome nose. He ignored it.

Then a metal claw clamped onto the rail. Painted wood squeaked as the serrated pincers sank into the wood.

Another claw did the same. Followed by two more.

Metal joints—long unlubricated, from the sound they made—rasped, levering the mechanical monster up.

A head appeared, peeping over the rail. Leastwise, it looked more like a head than much else. It was a polished cylindrical protrusion, like the tip of an enormous bullet. And featureless, save for a grilled voicebox and three glowing lenses which obviously served the machine creature as camera eyes. One shone red, another green; the middle one was yellow.

Grrff, Ganelon and Zarcas glared at the monster, attempting to look as threatening as possible under the circumstances. The three eyes glowed back, hopefully.

"Am sentient mechanoid, desirous of succor," the metal man informed them in a voice that was both hollow and tinny. "Also requiring loan of petroleum products. Am intending no harm to nice humanoids inadvertently frightened by sudden appearance of self. . . ."

"Avast and belay, you iron-covered land-lubber," began Zarcas. in his most ominous tones and in the approved piratical fashion.

"Am not understanding how to 'avast and belay,' " squeaked the mechanical man anxiously. "Self assures kindly humanoids it would be pleased to avast, also to belay; am requiring instruction in these undoubtedly interesting arts—"

Grrff, who was scared stiff, suddenly loosed a thunderous roar and clashed the hooked blades of his ygdraxel. Zarcas jumped nervously, and cursed at him. The Tigerman grinned back sheepishly. The mechanical man had ducked his head down at the roar, and now his voice echoed faintly from below deck level.

". . . Petroleum products? . . ."

He sounded rather mournful.

"Wait a minute, you big lugs," snapped Dalassa from behind them. She sounded exasperated. "I think you're frightening the poor thing."

"Wha's wrong wif that?" growled Grrff. "*He's* frightenin' *us*."

"Bu I don't believe the poor creature means us any harm —do you, metal man? Tell Dalassa what you want . . ."

Her voice had softened to a motherly croon. At this, the mechanoid timidly peeped up over the rail again, obviously ready to duck down if Grrff should roar again.

"Am meaning no harm to fellow sentients, lady," the mechanoid said weakly. "Self urgently requires petroleum products for lubrication of moving parts. Also am desirous of succor and rescue. Have been marooned on jungle island for ten million years. Self was former Tracking Station Attendant of Automatic Observatory F-109-X, situated atop Mount Korscio . . ."

"Well, I don't know what you're talking about, but for goodness sake stop dangling there like a gourd on the vine, and come aboard. You're beginning to bend the rail." Dalassa bustled forward to lend the mechanoid assistance.

"I say," remarked Zarcas to no one in particular. "Whose bloody ship *is* this, anyway? Inviting monsters aboard without so much as a by-your-leave . . . !"

"Oh, shut up," snapped Dalassa. "Where's your sense of hospitality, anyway?"

Zarcas stiffened. "My sense of hospitality, madame," he said thinly, "does not extend to mechanical monsters left over from previous epochs!"

"Oh, hush," said Dalassa, helping the timid mechanoid to the deck. "Poor thing, ten million years, you said? Poor little fellow must be lonely, nobody to talk to but those fat green hussies with the pink hair; I think it's a crying shame!"

She was clucking soothingly, not unlike a mother hen. The metal man eyed her shyly, gratitude shining in his triple eye-lamps.

"Very nice lady," he observed. "Zork Aargh no hurt nobody, unless nice lady tell him to."

Ganelon, Zarcas and Grrff exchanged helpless glances, and relaxed, and put away their weapons.

". . .*Wimmen!*" remarked the Tigerman, succintly.

"It's all over, so you can come out now, my brave boys," called Zarcas with a touch of sarcasm. One by one the pirates appeared from their hiding places.

"Jus' checkin' th' *hold*, Cap'n," boomed One-Eye self-consciously.

"And a good thing you did," murmured Zarcas with a delicate, aristocratic sneer. "Delighted to learn it is still there."

"Ever'thang shipshape aloft, Capting!" sang out Squint with attempted nonchalance, descending from the top of the mast.

"Be hit gone yit?" inquired Claw, his stalk-eyes peering fearfully out of the empty barrel in which the lobsterman was hiding.

"With a crew of fighting men like this, a man could conquer the world," groaned Zarcas the Zirian.

It took them a while to coax Ishgadara down; she had taken to the air and circled at three thousand feet until all was over.

By the time everything was quiet again, and the pirates were assured their peculiar new shipmate was a jolly swab, the *Bucket o' Blood* weighed anchor and stood to the wind, heading out to sea with the other ships in the flotilla trailing in her wake.

Dalassa had begged some lubricating oil and graphite from ship's stores, and solicitously helped the metal man sooth the friction in his joints. They had not rusted—the alloy whereof his form had anciently been fabricated was non-rusting—but centuries of grit and friction made them squeak and squeal terribly. Otherwise, he seemed in excellent condition, for a machine of his years.

Over dinner in the captain's cabin that night, the adventurers succeeded in piecing together the mechanoid's amazing history. He was the last (*probably* the last, at any rate) of an immense horde of robotic servitors invented by the technarchs of Vandalex, a long-extinct civilization which had flourished in the far west of the Supercontinent innumerable eons before. In that era the Technarchs of Vandalex had established heavily automated observatories on mountain peaks scattered about the less populated parts of Gondwane the Great, with mechanoids to tend to them and effect such repairs and refurbishings as might be necessary.

Well, sir, Grand Phesion fell about ten million years ago (give or take a dozen millennia) and Vandalexian civilization itself perished in conflict against the High Advocates of Tring. But nobody informed the robots, who continued to tend their machines in whatever remote outpost they had been assigned. Zork Aargh (for this seemed to be the name by which the robot attendant of Automatic Observatory F-109-X thought of himself) became aware at length that something had gone wrong with the ordinary nature of things. This was not until after geological forces created the Inland Sea of Zelphodon out of what had originally been a dreary wilderness. Further convulsions of nature reduced Mount Korscio to the lowly status of a mere island amidst the Sea.

Zork Aargh promptly reported these matters to the Central Intelligence which, presumably, monitored all robot communications. No further instructions were received by the poor little robot beyond those originally issued to him when the station was first established. Eventually, when the Observatory was completely vaporized by a direct hit—probably a meteorite of contraterrene matter—and no change in his instructions was given after he reported the fact, the mechanoid sensibly decided that the Eon of the Flying Cities had ended and the civilization which he had been created to serve was no more.

Zork Aargh had stayed on the island, since there was no

way for him to leave it without trying to walk across the sea bottom, whose squishy ooze would probably have swallowed him up and immobilized him, even if the moisture had not blown his circuits. His nuclear battery had a half-life of sixty million years, so he could look forward to an interminable existence of unmitigated monotony.

Sensibly adapting his radionic senses to the wavelengths of human speech, the mechanoid picked up a smattering of Gondwanish from eavesdropping on the lady savages who in time came to inhabit the isle. When ships of the Bloody Brotherhood began to land annually for the ritual plunder-and-parenthood, the mechanoid realized escape was at hand. It took the robot some years to figure out the precise periodicity of these yearly landings. When Zarcas' flotilla beached, therefore, Zork Aargh was ready to beg rescue.

Once they had gotten over their fear of the mechanical man, Zarcas and his pirate crew found him a congenial shipmate—and really not all that much odder than, say, Claw or Patch or One-Eye.

He stood about five-foot-seven, with a rounded, bulbous body of gleaming bright blue metal. Four thin, three-jointed legs protruded from the lower parts of his indigo body, evenly spaced about his lower perimeter. (Zork Aargh could, believe it or not, run either backwards or forwards with equal agility, without turning around; the trouble was, his eyes were all in the front and when he ran backwards he tended to fall over things a lot.)

He had four arms, similarly spaced about his upper torso, and likewise triply-jointed, which terminated in steely-toothed mandibles like the jaws on the business end of a wrench—and, in fact, designed to serve the identical purpose.

These mandibular "hands" could be disconnected and replaced with a variety of other tools, screwdrivers, power drills, and the like, all of which Zork Aargh kept packed away in the storage compartment situated in his tummy. Or where his tummy would be if he had one—but *you* know what I mean!

Anyway—despite his short size and rather comical appearance (the grill of his voicebox and his three round lens-eyes made him look pop-eyed and open-mouthed, as if he were in a continual state of surprise), Zork Aargh quickly became popular among his new friends and shipmates. Inoffensive, unassertive, and very anxious to please, the little automaton required neither rest, food nor sleep. He could work at some dreary shipboard task like painting the hull, patching sails, or scrubbing the deck, for days and nights without a break, and with, of course, the tireless efficiency of a machine. He never quarreled or got drunk or gambled or got lazy or stole or became ill. And he loved nothing more than standing nightwatch: then he was alone with ship and sea and starry sky, and he would solemnly stroll the deck, humming a queer little robotic tune to himself, dreaming of the good old days back in Vandalex.

Such was Zork Aargh.

But it did take the pirates a while to get used to having him aboard. In fact they did not fully become accustomed to Zork until they arrived at Zingaree, eight days' sail due west of Korscio.

They hove to in sight of the atoll at dawn on the ninth day, and the pirates eagerly clustered at the rail in all their buccaneering finery, happy to be going ashore.

Zork Aargh was the last to emerge from below decks. The little mechanoid, anxious to be accepted by his shipmates, had obviously gone to considerable effort to become one of them. At the very sight of him, they stopped short and stared.

Dalassa gasped in amazement, but managed to stifle her involuntary fit of giggles by turning it into a fit of coughing.

"Well, I'll be blowed!" swore One-Eye in his deep voice.

"Lamp the little lubber, willya, matey?" said Patch wonderingly to Squint.

"Zork, ya do be a sight," chuckled Squint, admiringly.

"Am looking all right . . .?" inquired the robot, anxiously.

"Ya look bee-*ooo*-tyful," grinned Squint.

And indeed he did! Zork Aargh had wound a scarlet kerchief about the top of his indigo cylindrical head, affixed two gold ear-hoops to the side of that protuberance with blobs of solder, tied a cloth-of-gold sash about the midpart of his globular torso, thrust it full of dirks and dags, and had put four floppy-topped sea boots on his four jointed metal legs, holding them on with rivets.

"Zorky, ye look ivvery *inch* a pirate," said Claw kindly.

"Thanking you muchly. . . . 'matey,'" said the mechanoid shyly.

From then on, he was just one of the crew.

10.

THE OOKABOOLAPONGA ON THE WARPATH

Having arrived at Zingaree, the pirates sailed into the atoll. And it was here that Zork Aargh found a chance to demonstrate his value to his shipmates.

The atoll was a mere wisp of land, interspersed with lots of green seawater. So little dry land was there for Zingaree to boast of, that most of the huts of the islanders were built over the water on piles. Hummocks and hillocks of sandy beach, naked rock and tree-grown soil were scattered about; but the place was mostly water.

Rather shallow water, obviously, for the adventurers could see the island folk walking about on stilts which enabled them to maintain their equilibrium whether on land or water. And some of them wore cork floats tied to the bottoms of their feet.

The atoll was a colorful, even a picturesque, place. Rattan huts stood out of the water, festooned with bright pink flowers; curious trees, rooted in the shallows, were draped with drifting beards of gray moss. Teetering, narrow catwalks connected the huts: the village seemed to hover halfway between sea and sky. A bit farther off, in the background, the main body of land, a crescent of shaggy swamp, appeared like a tangled mangrove.

The natives were small folk, timid, anxious to be friendly. They were also naked, except that men and women alike wore bright pink flowers woven in their hair. They had amber skin and luxurious black hair, oiled and scented, and they conversed in a musical, sing-song variant of Gondwanish that was pretty to listen to but a little hard to understand until you got used to it. It was a dialect which Ganelon Silvermane had never heard.

When the ships came cruising into the central bay, the islanders came out happily, waving and calling soft greetings, throwing flowers. Drums pattered; bonfires were lit on floating platforms of wood; a feast was promptly thrown to welcome the visitors.

This unusual hospitality rather nonplussed the buccaneers. Previously, when they had descended upon Zingaree to raid and loot and plunder, the islanders had run into the swamp to hide. But now they seemed delighted to see the pirates.

They came out to meet the ships, some stalking along on stilts, others walking on their pontoon-like floats, many in slim-hulled canoes. They grinned and chattered shyly, handing up wreaths of flowers and noggins of fermented coconut milk and ripe pawpaws to the bewildered buccaneers, who crowded the rail, ogling the bare pointed breasts of the little brown women.

Black Horrog and Zarcas, in their gigs, went ashore to treat with the chief of the Zingareeans, a fat, affable, smiling, lazy fellow named Okk. They soon returned, laden with pearls and bags of loot, with the news that the Zingareeans had invited them all to a feast that evening. They were still in the dark as to why the islanders were so friendly this time, when last time they had all scurried away to hide in the mangroves.

Docking their ships at the end of rickety little wooden piers, the pirates traded glass beads and mirrors with the islanders for native crafts—carved nuts, ivory scrimshaw, quaint little idols of polished mangananga wood and the like. Some of them ambled ashore with one or two giggling native girls to enjoy the ultimate in hospitality. The Zingaree men didn't seem to mind at all.

It was curious, but rather nice. The pirates of Zarcas' crew were, on the whole, a soft-hearted, good-natured lot who would rather trade and wheedle for loot than seize it. It's more fun to accept gifts than fight for them.

With late afternoon the feast commenced. Seasnake shish-kebab, toasted rice cakes, fresh fish wrapped in palm leaves and broiled over hissing coals, and huge crisp salads spiced with exotic sliced fruit—and, of course, copious draughts of the heady native drink.

Bonfires roared, lighting the darkening village with orange flaring light. Drums pattered, cymbals tinkled, native girls performed lissom, swaying, languorous dances which set piratical pulses throbbing louder than the drums. Zarcas himself vanished into one of the high huts with two nubile native girls; Dalassa looked sour and returned to her cabin aboard ship, claiming a headache.

She returned almost instantly, wild-eyed. The ships were swarming with blue-painted natives wearing war plumes, armed with spiked wooden clubs and long, wicked-looking spears, she announced. They had come aboard from forty outrigger canoes, swarming over the sides. But they didn't look like the men of Zingaree.

They weren't, Ukk informed them solemnly.

"Them is Ookaboolaponga," the chief said sadly. "Ever' year this time them raids us. Us hoped mebbe-so pirates'd scare um off. Guess us figgered wrong. Too bad. Have um more pawpaw wine?"

"Wine?" snarled Grrff testily. "We gotta get them ships back or we're gonna git marooned here fer th' rest o' our natural lives!"

Kurdi, exchanging fascinated glances with a slender little dark-eyed island girl about his own age, privately thought that would not be the worst of imaginable fates. But Ganelon was as perturbed as Grrff, and quickly roused Zarcas from his hut in mid-revel. Frowning with annoyance, the corsair appeared in the doorway, demanding to know who had disturbed him. From his state of undress, and the two island girls clinging to him, the reason for his annoyance was easy to guess.

Dalassa sniffed and looked away frostily.

Once Ganelon had told him what was up, Zarcas looked alarmed, disentangled himself from the two amorous native girls, searched around, found his trousers and sword belt, and clambered down the ladder to begin kicking and rousing his men from their drowsy or drunken stupor.

"The Ookaboolaponga are on the warpath," he informed Black Horrog, rudely waking him up.

"Th' who?" Horrog inquired groggily.

"The Ookaboolaponga," stated Zarcas crisply. "They live on the Ookaboolaponga Islands, somewhere over that way. They have nobody else to go to war against on their own islands, so about once a year they row over here to loot, plunder and ravish the Zingaree girls."

"Thass *awful*," growled Horrog indignantly, his pockets stuffed with pearls, shoving away the two native girls he had earlier ravished himself, "Sumphin oughta be done about *thet*."

"Something will," promised Zarcas grimly, going off to find Patch and Squint and One-Eye.

It took Zarcas a while to locate all of his men and to marshall those of them who were not too drunk to stand into some kind of fighting order.

It took Black Horrog a trifle longer to do the same, considering his handicap—he had imbibed a bit freely of fermented coconut milk and pawpaw wine, and was more than a bit rubbery in the legs while someone seemed to have established a boiler factory behind his forehead.

Finally, the pirates were ready (more or less) for the rather tricky business of attempting to recapture their ships. The two lesser captains of the flotilla, Vlasko and Zollobus, doubted it could be done without the assistance of the Zingareeans. Vlasko was particularly vehement on that point.

"But they aren't fighters," argued Zarcas. "The easy island life has made them soft and lazy. They do nothing but lie around all day wearing flowers, getting drunk, and making love. The moment the Ookaboolaponga showed up, they began drifting off into the shadows. Look around you—there's not a Zingareean in sight except those who are too drunk to stand up."

"The lad be right, Vlasko," chirped Zollobus, puffing out his cheeks and glaring across the water. "Them spineless goops be no doubt hidin' back in thet swamp: well, an' who needs 'em, sez I. Our lads be hale an' hearty, more'n enough t' settle the hash o' them savages!"

Vlasko looked dubious; he snorted, bristling his enormous mustachios like a bull walrus at bay.

"We-uns be needin' ivvry stout hand as kin be mustered," he muttered. "Le's go root 'em outa thet swamp, Zolly—a taste o' steel, *thass* what they be needin'—"

"No time fer thet, cuss yew," growled Black Horrog, hefting his nicked and dented scimitar. "Any moment now them Ookaboolypongies c'd cut th' anchor lines an' sail away, leavin' us here wiff nothink t' do but futter island girls an' git fat. Le's go git um!"

"I greatly fear Horrog is right," said Zarcas. "It's now or never. My boys will board the *Bucket*, while you captains

lead your own crews to the rescue of your own ships. Ready?
Follow me, lads—"

All did not go well with the rescue, gallant try though it
was. For one thing, the Falling Moon had not yet risen and
the sky being overcast, the night was a dark one. It is asking
a bit much of pirates who had perhaps taken aboard a few
noggins of fermented coconut milk too many to be able to
negotiate the narrow and rickety little wooden-slat piers with
any nimbleness or facility. More than a few fell off it, and
One-Eye, who was heavier than most of the crew, fell
through it and got stuck. He dangled there squalling, his
cyclops-eye rolling about fearfully. It took three men to pry
him loose and haul him back up.

While the passageway was blocked in this manner some of
the more intrepid buccaneers decided to board the vessel by
means of devices uniquely Zingareean. But they were a little
too rubbery in the knees to be able to scoot along atop the
water on the cork floats the natives use, and they were *very*
awkward on stilts. Most of them fell in and floundered in the
shallows, howling until dragged out of the drink by their
shipmates.

None of them could swim.

Zarcas swore furiously, looking harried. His men were
making more than enough noise to wake the dead, much less
rouse the Ookaboolaponga. Eventually he pummeled and
pushed them into line and they negotiated the wobbly little
pier without further mishap. Swarming up over the side of
their ship, they stopped short and gaped in amazement at the
scene which met their eyes.

The decks were littered with unconscious Ookaboolapongas.

Some had black eyes, others bloody noses, and more than
a few cracked ribs or lumps on their heads.

All, however, were definitely *hors de combat*.

"Am welcoming shipmates aboard," sang out a familiar
tinny voice. "Self will have things shipshape in proverbial
jiffy."

Zarcas rubbed his eyes and looked again.

Zork Aargh had not, after all, gone ashore for long. The
little mechanoid could neither eat nor drink nor fool around
with native girls, so had early become bored with the festivities and decided to return to the *Bucket o' Blood* and relieve
the watch. When the savages had come creeping over the

side, his electronic senses had long known of their approach, and the robot pirate pitched in without further ado.

He might be short and bulbous and faintly comical, but he could certainly fight. Those four metal arms of his were fearful weapons in the fray, knocking savages left and right, head over heels into the gunwales. Nor could they injure the lone defender with their weaponry. Stone knives and wooden clubs and spears did no more than scratch the gleaming finish on his indigo hide.

Having knocked the savages silly, Zork Aargh went to the storeroom, emerged with coils of spare rope, and had been busily engaged in tying them all up when the boarding party arrived on the scene.

"My claws an' whiskers, Zork, yer a one-man army!" marveled Grrff.

"Shore glad we got yez on *our* side, matey!" swore Squint with earnest admiration.

"Yes, well done, little fellow," applauded Captain Zarcas feelingly. The others came crowding around to shake one or another of the mechanoid's four claws and clap him on the back.

Zork Aargh nearly burst his rivets with pride, expanding almost visibly under the compliments and admiration of his new friends.

From across the water, where the other ships of the flotilla were moored, came the sound of furious fighting. Ululating their savage war cries, the Ookaboolaponga fought the pirates tooth and nail. The clash of weapons, the grunt and scuffle of struggling men, and the occasional startled yelp—followed by a splash—as somebody fell overboard made the night, if not exactly hideous, at least noisy.

The toughest fight seemed to be aboard the *Black Bessie,* from which poor Horrog had already fallen overboard four times. Leaning comfortably against their rail, listening interestedly to the yowl and yammer, Zarcas and Squint, Grrff, Ganelon, Dalassa and Kurdi observed the waterlogged pirate scramble swearing and dripping back up the cable for the fourth time, and jump back into the battle.

"S'pose we sh'd go lend 'im a hand, Capting," murmured Squint dreamily.

"Probably," yawned the Zirian without moving.

Grrff chuckled: Horrog was a troublemaker and his dislike of the captives he had made blatantly obvious by many glares

and snorts, bad jokes and put-downs. The Tigerman felt no
burning need to go to his assistance; neither, it seemed, did
any of his fellow pirates, who seemed to be enjoying the
scene as much as Grrff.

"Betcha two gol' pieces he falls overboard agin," said
Patch to Claw.

"Three gol' pieces sez he gits dunked at *leas'* twicet," returned Claw, his stalk eyes gleaming with lazy satisfaction as
he listened to the lusty squalling from the other ship.

"Yer on," said Patch.

Both lost. Black Horrog landed in the lagoon three more
times before the *Black Bessie* was finally recaptured.

Late the next morning the four ships weighed anchor and
sailed from the lagoon of Zingaree.

The bedraggled, disgruntled, thoroughly unhappy savages,
stripped of their finery and all their weapons, were put back
in their canoes and permitted to row back to the Ookaboolaponga Islands.

Zarcas, Horrog, Zollobus and Vlasko went ashore to collect
those of their crews who had been too inebriated to fight the
night before and who had been left behind to sleep it off.

The timid little Zingaree islanders emerged from the
mangrove swamps where they had been hiding, to see them
off. They were very grateful and heaped the ships of the
flotilla with gifts and goodies.

Weighing anchor, the ships headed into the wind, bound
for Arjis Isle, their home port.

The expedition had not been such a failure, after all. Their
holds bulged with loot and plunder.

En route they sailed by the weary, headachy Ookaboolapongas, and razzed them unmercifully. The dispirited
savages wilted under the hooting mockery of their erstwhile
foes. But they did not have enough fight left in them to return the jibes.

It was much to be doubted that the Ookaboolapongas
would ever go on the warpath again.

If they ever did, it probably wouldn't be in the direction of
Zingaree.

Book Three

SILVERMANE ON ARJIS ISLE

The Scene: The Port of Orgaza on Arjis Isle in the Third Lesser Inland Sea of Zelphodon.

New Characters: Captains Vlasko and Zollobus; Raschid the Red; Various Members of the Bloody Brotherhood; Gyzik of Ziria.

11.

HORROG MAKES TROUBLE

Six days after setting sail from Zingaree, sailing south and east all the way, brought the pirate flotilla to Arjis Isle.

This large jungle island with its palm-fringed beaches and soaring volcanic peak in the center, was the headquarters and home port of the buccaneers of the Bloody Brotherhood.

The isle was inhabited only by pirates, and was under their rule. Oh, there were a few runaway slaves, escaped captives and various assorted savages hiding out in the jungles, but nobody paid much attention to *them*. Not counting runaways and riffraff, the corsairs ruled their own kingdom and had the final say as to what was what.

This was certainly convenient. Elsewhere upon the high seas and shores and islands of the mighty Zelphodon they were criminals, outlaws, sea-brigands. Ships flying the Bloody Banner were fair game. Known pirates were strung up on gibbets whenever captured.

But Arjis Isle was the corsairs' own kingdom: here they made the laws. And the very first law they passed was to make piracy as legal as any other profession (like loan-sharking or being a lawyer).

The pirate kingdom, however, had no king. This was mainly because the buccaneers were a wary, suspicious lot, each jealous of his own reputation and thus unwilling to let any other pirate lord it over him.

In theory, at least, this was so. In practice, however, a realm needs a firm hand at the helm, so to speak. Someone to see that the Articles are enforced, loot is divided fairly, trai-

93

tors, thieves and murderers get their just desserts, and the affairs of the corsair kingdom are ably conducted.

So the buccaneers elected a Chief every three years by secret ballot.

The current chief, one Raschid the Red, had been in office for more than two and a half years now. He secretly lusted for a second term. Not that it was much of a secret.

It was to Raschid's palace that Black Horrog went just as fast as his furry legs could carry him, once the *Black Bessie* was snugly moored. The redbeard bore a grudge against Ganelon and the others for slicing up his crew in the attack on Urgoph. And his temper had not exactly been sweetened much by recent events: he had seen them grinning at the rail every time he had fallen overboard in the fight to recapture his ship from the Ookaboolapongas.

Horrog, grinning nastily as he trotted through the crooked streets of Orgaza, thought that Raschid would be interested to know that Zarcas had become quite chummy with the captives. This was mainly because the rakish young daredevil was very popular with the buccaneers of Arjis Isle and Raschid was by now heartily disliked. And if Zarcas should decide to run against Raschid in the coming elections. . . .

He was right, was Horrog.

Raschid *was* interested: *very* interested.

The capital of the corsair kingdom was a cluttered, gaudy little town built on the slopes of the volcano which dominated the island.

It had crooked, narrow, twisting streets that wound between houses and taverns, mostly of two-stories and mostly of stucco, painted pink and yellow and blue and pistachio green, with red tile roofs and wooden signs swinging over the doors.

Some of them were dilapidated and run-down, the stucco badly in need of painting and cracked here and there. The narrow streets and dark alleys were choked with garbage and awash with stinking mud, which oozed in fetid streams between the greasy cobbles.

Orgaza had thirty rooming houses and ninety-eight taverns, wineshops, beer halls, gambling casinos, bordellos, flophouses and other establishments which purveyed the pleasures of the flesh.

It had eight larger and rather palatial houses, with walled gardens and courtyards, the property of the more important and successful and, therefore, richer captains.

The largest and fanciest of them all was the Residence, where the Chief held court.

There were many shops along the seafront: chandlers, ship carpenters, sellers of maps and nautical instruments, slave markets, tanners, dyers, amulet sellers, blacksmiths, jewelers, pawn shops, fortune tellers, tattoo shops, clothiers, and merchants of one kind or another.

Ganelon and his friends debarked from the *Bucket o' Blood*. Grrff looked about him warily, not much liking what he saw. Dalassa was disdainful and glanced about with a sniff of disapproval. Drunks sprawled in gutters, urchins ran shrieking at nameless games; three fist fights were in progress; slatternly, heavily painted women called from second-floor windows, lewdly beckoning; beggars whined on street corners; panderers leered and lurked in dark alley mouths. The harbor wasn't much to look at.

"I'm going to put you up with Zollobus and Vlasko," muttered Zarcas. "They have rooms over the Jolly Roger."

"Whyzat?" grumbled Grrff.

"Because Black Horrog hotfooted it to the Residence as quick as he could, doubtless to make trouble," said Zarcas grimly. "He thinks I'm too easy on captives—too soft-hearted to make a real pirate. If I put you up in my house, it will look as though I *am* coddling you."

"Told ya we'd have trouble from that 'un," growled the Tigerman to his friend. Ganelon nodded thoughtfully.

"You'll be comfortable enough, I'm sure," said Zarcas, strolling away into the crowd.

"A lot *he* cares," sniffed Dalassa, trying not to look miserable. Grrff snorted at her affectionately.

"Kinda putcher nose outa joint," grinned the Karjixian, "when Cap'n Zarc' entertained them two island ladies, eh?"

The blonde girl looked indignant, but she was trying to look incredulous.

"*Me?*" she inquired, as if amazed that Grrff should entertain such a notion. "Whatever gave you the idea that I could possibly—!—I mean, if I ever for one moment—! Honestly, where you men get your crazy ideas—!"

Grrff chuckled, but knew when to clam up.

The Jolly Roger was a noisy little tavern on a side street off the harbor. The taproom was long, low-ceilinged, with smoke-blackened rafters, long wine-spotted tables crowded with raffish mariners, and a roaring fire on the grate, where a huge side of yikyik steak sizzled odorously on a spit. Vlasko

and fat little Zollobus were hailed with hearty greetings; nobody paid much attention to Silvermane and his friends.
Ishgadara waddled out to the stables to curl up on dry straw.

They dined sumptuously on dripping yikyik steaks, roast
rump of tree-dwelling elephant with ecstasy sauce, jungle-
berry salad, fried yams, mangoes stewed in beer, and hot bis-
cuits soaked in honey, and the feast was washed down with
copious draughts of hot spiced ale. Extra cots and mattresses
had been moved into the bachelor quarters the two corsair
captains maintained over the inn, and they slept soundly that
night, happy to have dry land under them again. Dalassa
alone did not sleep too well; obviously, the handsome pirate
chieftain with his reckless ways and swaggering manner had
gotten to the daughter of Borgo Methrix, no matter how she
tried to pretend they were mere acquaintances. A full month
of involuntary propinquity sometimes did such things, and
during the thirty days between their capture by the buccaneers and their arrival at Arjis Isle, she and the captain had
been much together.*

Next morning Zarcas the Zirian arrived to escort them to
the Residence where the ransom terms were to be discussed
and agreed upon. Raschid the Red was closeted with his
crony, Black Horrog, and when they emerged into the
Council Hall Ganelon and the others discovered the reason
for his appellation: he was bright scarlet all over, like stewed
tomatoes, with sharp green eyes that rather clashed with his
complexion.

"Ol' Raschid, y'know, he be's a Redman fum Kermish,"
confided little Zollobus in his deep foghorn voice. "Them-uns
be as red o' skin as stewed hukluks."

"Obviously," said Dalassa coolly, not caring for the way
the pirate king was ogling her contours.

"Quite a feller fer th' ladies, too," Vlasko pointed out,
rather unnecessarily.

---

* Glancing back over the earlier volumes of my prose redaction of the
Epic, I notice I have not gone into any detail concerning the Gondwanish calendar. Between our own era and that of Ganelon Silvermane, Old Earth has slightly accelerated in her annual orbit about
the Sun, and the Gondwanish year is therefore made up of 360 days,
divided into twelve months of exactly thirty days each.

The names of the different months vary according to place. But in
the Realm of the Nine Hegemons, where Ganelon was raised, they are
called Ruphad, Foche, Porchoy, Arb, Kallidon, Suchab, Stoy, Pharble,
Quine, Zulpha, Pernaby and Huk—with the year starting in the month
of Ruphad, or January. The seasons, however, are considerably different from ours.

Dalassa said nothing. Zarcas had greeted them with pretended coldness—barely nodding. However, when Raschid was not looking, he tipped the captives a broad wink and gave them a quick, surreptitious grin.

The terms for their ransom were agreed upon with little discussion, and by lunch time the document had been drawn up (on crisp parchment, in blood, scrawled all over with skulls and crossbones) and was dispatched by seamail back to Urgoph.

Seamail turned out to be just about what it sounded as if it might be, if you take my meaning. It seems the pirates and other human denizens of the Zelphodon Sea shared that body of water with a race of Merfolk who had immigrated to these waters about a generation ago. Their original home was in the Second Lesser Inland Sea of Quadquoph, over in the Conglomerate of Inner Pongolia, northwest of Lower Arzenia.

These displaced Pongolians were a green-blue, scaly lot, with goggling eyes and fishy fins, smaller, slimmer and stronger than most True Men. Genuine water breathers, they lived on the sea bottom in coral caverns and hunted sea snakes for a living, armed with their traditional mer-pikes, an aquatic weapon like a throwing-trident with hollow glass prongs filled with nerve poison which immobilized the sea snakes without killing them.

Unhappily—or perhaps "happily," as far as the humans who dwelt along the shores of the Zelphodon, and on its many islands, reefs, atolls and archipelagoes, were concerned—there are no sea snakes in the Zelphodon. So the finny immigrants had to find another way to earn a living in their new home.

They had hit upon the novel concept of delivering the mail. The Merfolk, although a bit sluggish and slow-thinking, were not by any means stupid: quite the opposite, they tended on the whole to be a clever lot. One particularly brainy Merperson, looking around for something the water dwellers could do better than their neighboring land dwellers, thought of a postal service. With their slim and powerful seahorses, called Campchurches, they could negotiate the depths far more swiftly and easily than the Zelphodonian mariners could sail the sea's surface.

Hence, seamail—a uniquely Zelphodonian phenomenon.

With the blood-written ransom-demand sealed in a watertight container, the pirates awaited the appearance of the mer-mailman, who soon arrived to make his afternoon deliveries. The document—superscribed to: His Munificence the Hon. Borgo Methrix, Grand Magnatorial Palace, Urgoph, North Shore—was popped in the Merperson's pouch, postage paid for in salted herrings, sea-figs and trade-silver, and the letter was on its way.

The reply was expected in about seven days.

"You gittin' any harrassment fum yer Chief, Cap'n Zarc'? inquired Grrff solicitously on the ride back from the Residence.

"No more than I had expected," said the Zirian airily. He was mounted on one of the amphibious nguamodons the folk of Arjis Isle employed in lieu of orniths*, while his four captives were riding on Ishgadara's back.

"Horrog would dearly love to make trouble for you," he added. "And Chief Rachid would enjoy making trouble for *me,* and would, if I weren't so popular with the voters." He explained in a careless tone about the coming elections.

Later that evening, after dinner, Grrff and Dalassa whispered together conspiratorially during a brief turn about the courtyard under the blazing stars. They returned to their quarters to put the escape proposition to Ganelon Silvermane squarely. Might as well have it out in the open.

"We ain't aboard th' *Bucket o' Blood* now, big man, so yer promise t' Cap'n Zarc' not to run off is, um, whatchacallit—?" said Grrff the Xombolian.

"—Invalid?" suggested Dalassa.

"Mebbe . . . (thought that meant somebody as wuz *sick*) . . . anyways, no reason why we sh'unt take off on Ishy's back and fly backta Urgoph," argued the Tigerman.

"Hmm," Silvermane considered.

"We would be doing my father a favor," put in the blonde girl. "He's going to hate coming up with all that trade-silver."

"Yeah," grumbled Grrff, "Ol' Raschid *did* demand a hefty price fer our carcasses."

"*I'd* pay all m' wealth t' rescue *you* from trouble," said Kurdi, looking dreamily up at the blonde-haired beauty. Kurdi was at that age when older women are fascinating creatures, being unplumbed mysteries.

---

* The salty sea air was bad for the Gondwanish bird-horses and made them moult their feathers, which put them in a bad temper and made them generally intractable—says the Fourteenth Commentary at this point, and Glundalclitch is rarely wrong.

"Aw, you're sweet," giggled Dalassa, tousling his hair affectionately. Then, more practically: "But what do you say, Ganelon? We could make our escape tonight, and I could be home by morning—Well, just about."

"There are two problems you haven't considered, Dalassa," said Silvermane woodenly.

"There are, are there?"

"Yes. For one thing, we have been disarmed, and I have no idea where they have put our weapons and gear for safekeeping," Ganelon pointed out. "Grrff is accustomed to his ygdraxel, and would feel like a Merperson out of water without it."

"Thass true, ol' Grrff's gotta admit it," sighed the Karjixian. "Ain't likely t' find another this side o' Northern YamaYamaLand, either. . . ."

Ganelon, you will notice, refrained from adding that he would heartily miss the Silver Sword, his own famous weapon. It had been a gift to him from the grateful people of the Hegemony on the occasion of his Triumph, in reward for his beating off the Indigons. He had never been without it since, and as it had been made especially for him by Fire Magic, there was no other broadsword like it in all of Gondwane.

"All right, I'll buy that," said Dalassa, gloomily. "What's the *other* problem involved in our getting out of here?"

Silvermane called to their attention the predicament in which their escape would place Zarcas the Zirian. It was widely known that he had befriended them during the long voyage from Urgoph to Arjis Isle. His complicity in their escape would definitely be suspected.

"We owe the captain something," said Silvermane. "He could have chained us in our cabin, or locked us in the hold. Instead we dined at the captain's table and were treated more than just decently, but with genuine hospitality. I will not escape at this time if to do so will reflect suspicion upon Zarcas or imperil him in any way."

There was grim finality in his tone as he made that remark. And they all knew that when Ganelon Silvermane said something with that ring of somber decision in his voice there was no changing his mind.

"So much fer escape," sighed Grrff, bedding down for the night. "Le's sure hope yer dad comes up wif th' ransom money!"

"I'm sure he will," said Dalassa confidently, snuggling into her pillow on the other side of the curtain which gave her privacy. But inwardly she was not all that confident. It was not that familial feelings did not exist among the Urgovians, it was that the Magnates worried first about their fortunes before giving thought to their offspring.

After all, too, she was only her father's second daughter and eleventh child.

Well, they would have to wait and see. . . .

12.
ZOLLOBUS SPILLS THE BEANS

During the next week, while awaiting the reply from Urgoph to the ransom demand, the adventurers became acquainted with Orgaza.

They were not kept under any particular surveillance and were permitted to go wherever they wished. The reason for the unusual freedom of movement afforded the prisoners was, quite simply, that Arjis Isle itself was one large prison for them. There was no way to leave the island unless aboard one of the pirate ships—and five escaping prisoners are not enough to sail a ship, even if they were able and lucky enough to manage to steal one.

There only remained Ishgadara, their last hope of escape. Unfortunately, the lady sphinx was quite effectively "grounded," for the pirates had clipped her lead feathers. Lacking them she could not fly well enough to transport them any particular distance. And the missing feathers would not grow back for several weeks.

"Shoulda skipped out when we had th' chance," grumbled Grrff.

"Too late now," sighed Dalassa.

Each day during the wait they were guests at dinner, their hosts being one or another of the Captains. There were ten of these gentry in the Council, which was the principal deliberative body in the government of Arjis, serving as advisors to Raschid, who was himself the first and foremost of the Captains.

The second in Council was a bluff, brawling fellow called Wargo, or Skull Wargo, because of his shaven pate. He was

101

rough and boisterous, and second in pelf, popularity and prestige only to Raschid himself. Third in line was a strange little man called Scrimshaw, who had been a sailing captain in the ivory trade down along the South Shore of Zelphodon. He had hunted sea unicorns for their spiral-fluted ivory horns, and Behemoths for their enormous tusks. The reason for his nickname was that during these voyages, before turning to a life of piracy, Scrimshaw had suffered the loss of one leg and also of his left hand. These missing members had been replaced by artificial ones carved from the ivory horns and tusks of the sea beasts, which Scrimshaw had decorated with quaint designs to while away the lonely weeks at sea.

Black Horrog was accounted the fourth of the Captains and Zarcas the Zirian was the fifth. The sixth was considered to be an enormously fat Clovian named Baba the Barbarous, followed by Zarcas' good friends Vlasko and Zollobus and two lesser Captains, Gronk and Illibis. Gronk was a savage from the Kakkawakka Islands with file teeth and frizzled hair, while Illibis was a tightmouthed, close-fisted, scrawny little Soormian renegade.

This rotation of hosts was so that the prisoners should not get too chummy with any of the Captains.

The two they saw the most of were Zollobus and Vlasko. In public these two pretended to dislike guests foisted upon them, but actually they became the best of friends.

Vlasko was a dour old salt, lean in the shanks and long in the arms, with a grizzled, gray-shot beard and shrewd yellow eyes. He was sour of temper and gruff of speech, but this was a facade erected to keep folks from discovering that he was really kind and softhearted. He also boasted an enormous walrus mustache, which was his pride and joy. Kurdi adored him, and the two would spend hours exploring the wharves while the dour old seaman spun wild yarns of blood-thirsty sea battles for the amusement of the wide-eyed youngster.

Zollobus was as squat and broad as Vlasko was tall and skinny. The pair of them, seen together, always made Grrff chuckle: they reminded him of Palensus Choy and pudgy little Ollub Vetch, whom they had not seen now for many months.

Zollobus had bright blue skin and was an Azdrugian. Azdruga was a small, seafaring country on the western shore of the Zelphodon, near the border of Inner Pongolia. Zollobus had very short legs, and was very fat, and walked with a waddling gait that Kurdi found comical. Also, he had pop-eyes in his fat-cheeked moon-face which gave him a comical expression.

These two were the particular friends of Zarcas because, like him, they were rather too tender-hearted and not blood-thirsty enough to be very good pirates. Zarcas was considered a comer among the Captains of the Bloody Brotherhood because he was remarkably lucky and his exploits and piratical ventures generally paid off handsomely.

But he was really not a pirate at all.

He was a Prince in disguise.

This secret came out one evening during the week they were waiting for the reply to come from Urgoph. The adventurers were being dined at the table of Zollobus, which was at his favorite cookhouse, the Gallumphing Gourmet.

This particular waterfront tavern was famous for its cuisine, and the fat little pirate was notoriously fond of the pleasures of the table. Its name derived from the peculiar mode of locomotion employed by the waiters, who were all quasi-intelligent Hoppers from the jungle isle of Skoor. Hoppers have three double-jointed legs and do not walk, jog, lope or gallop—they *gallumph.*

After a singularly succulent meal consisting of sea crabs boiled in white wine with gik-butter sauce, singe-fried orotolans, Ooo Soup (the chef's specialty) and gungle-spice salad, Zollobus, having taken aboard a few too many tankards of grog, let slip the royal ancestry of Zarcas.

Immediately, he blushed with guilt. (When a blue-skinned Azdrugian blushes, by the way, he turns royal purple.)

"Fergit whut I said," boomed the fat captain, glaring around belligerently in his pop-eyed way. "Zarcas'll have me liver out ta feed the crows!"*

But Dalassa, curious and heartily intrigued by this chance disclosure, wheedled and coaxed and flattered the whole story out of him. This was not hard to do, as the remarkably beautiful blonde girl was, as usual, wearing remarkably little in the way of clothing. And Zollobus rather fancied himself a ladies' man, and was quite susceptible to blondes.

It seems that Zarcas was the third son of Zaractacas, former King of Ziria. Ziria was a rich and powerful kingdom over in Southern YamaYamaLand, at the eastern edge of the Sea of

* A deliberate mistranslation. Zollobus actually referred to punky-punky birds, which are notorious garbage scavengers. I simply cannot continue to interrupt the smooth flow of my narrative with these everlasting footnotes!

Zelphodon. The Sea, you understand—and if you haven't yet looked at the frontispiece map, please do so, although it won't show Ziria—was large and long, so long that one third of it extended over the border of Lower Arzenia into Southern YamaYamaLand.

But I digress. Ten years before, when Zarcas had been about sixteen, his royal father had been murdered by one of his uncles, Urzang the Usurper, aided in his nefarious plots by a powerful sorcerer. Not only had King Zaractacas been done away with, but also his two eldest sons, Zaragon and Zaraka. The Usurper had then . . . ah . . . ursurped the throne of Ziria, executing or imprisoning all of the Peers whom he believed to be friendly with the Royalist Faction. These he replaced with a seedy gang of his own cronies, henchmen, toadies and hangers-on.

But he had overlooked one Royalist, a sea captain named Zollobus.

He also failed to get into his clutches the youngest son of the liquidated monarch, Prince Zarcas, who had been away in the hills on a hunting trip with an old family retainer called Vlasko. The two faithful friends had smuggled the boy out of Ziria, and, with the aid of one of their friends among the pirates (none other than Scrimshaw, who had but recently turned to the piratical life) they hid him among the corsairs of Arjis Isle.

Raised to be a pirate, he had in time become one. At times, memories of his former state tormented him, and Zarcas fell into melancholy moods. Also, now and again, the fact that he had not yet avenged the honor of his family by slaying the Usurper rankled deeply, and he became grim and brooding.

"And has Zarcas never attempted to return and to revenge his father's murder upon the Usurper and the sorcerer?" inquired Dalassa breathlessly.

Zollobus shook his head.

"Fer whut—t' git hisself kilt, too?" asked the fat pirate argumentatively. "Not much one pirate kin do aginst a whole *navy*, y'know, missy! An' Ziria is got th' bigges' and bestes' navy in all these-here parts. . . ."

Going back to their quarters that night, under the splendor of the Falling Moon, Dalassa was curiously silent. Usually, she talked their heads off; but from her dreamy expression and languid eyes, and the occasional deep sighs she sighed, they understood the reason for her un-Dalassa-like mood.

She was a thorough romantic at heart, was Dalassa.

And Zarcas was very handsome.

Somehow, the fact that he was a Prince-in-Exile made him even handsomer. ...

The next morning, Ganelon found an opportunity to talk about these matters with grizzled old Vlasko.

The dour old salt grinned nastily, whuffing out his walrus mustache.

"So Zolly spilled ther beans, did 'ee?" cackled Vlasco. "Dang fool nivver c'ud hold 'is liquor. 'Grog'll be yer doom an' downfall' *I* allers sez. If'n I sez hit oncet, I sez it t' 'im a thousing times. ..."

"But does anyone here on Arjis Isle know the Captain's secret?" asked Silvermane. The old sailor shrugged his skinny shoulders.

"Nupe. But ther do be them as *suspec's*," he muttered ominously. "Thet red-bearded hog, Horrog, fer one ..."

"What about back in Ziria?" inquired Grrff, who had accompanied Ganelon on his morning stroll.

The mustached mariner grinned hugely, displaying a gold tooth.

"Pore ol' Urzang 'ees searched high an' low fer y'ars and y'ars," chuckled the pirate. "Ivver nook 'n' cranny in Ziria. An' 'is spies 'ave combed ivver kingdom fer twenny countries 'round. Mus' be purty deesprit by now, I cal'clate! But nivver a trace o' th' lad c'ud ee find. No idee th' lad be struttin' around here in Arjis, big as big an' bold as bold."

Then his canny yellow eyes narrowed shrewdly, and his voice fell to a hoarse whisper.

"If'n thet dang Usurper ivver finds out th' lad be here, 'ee'll 'ave 'is whole dang navy out, an' we-uns'll 'ave a *war* on our hands, yew mind ma words, fellers!"

Little did any of them think that the warning Vlasko uttered that day was a prophecy, soon to come true.

But they had other things to worry about besides the secret of Zarcas the Zirian.

For one thing, this was the morning of the *eighth* day. Which meant Urgoph was late in responding to the ransom demand. This was just a trifle odd, the lateness in reply I mean, for seamail was in general very reliable: the Merfolk had little else to do but deliver the mail, and were zealous in maintaining their reputation for prompt, unerring deliveries. "Nor muck of bottom nor storm of surface shall stay these couriers from the swift completion of their appointed rounds," that was their motto.*

Silvermane and his friends were not exactly worried; any number of factors such as the weather, etc., could easily have delayed the return message by a day or two. But, when three days passed and no reply to the ransom demand arrived at Arjis Isle, things did begin to look a bit sticky.

There were mutterings in the Captains' Council, and Black Horrog, always the troublemaker, began loudly talking about "an example." His notion of a polite reminder to the Urgovians ran to things like a package containing the freshly-severed left *ears* of the captives, and similarly genteel mementoes designed to spur prompt response from the recalcitrant Magnate.

Luckily for our friends, these stern measures were soon proven unnecessary. Off-shore patrols reported the approach of a vessel flying the Urgovian colors—quace and dark talary, in alternating stripes. Speculation ran rife on the pirate isle: one ship was, of course, too small for an invasion; but certainly large enough to carry the ransom money.

By morning of the next day, the Urgovian galley hove to just beyond the harbor, and ran up signals requesting an Arjisian pilot be sent out to guide them in. The pirates (those that were sober enough, that is) all trooped down to the harbor front to watch the doings.

The harbor was, by the way, enclosed with two curving walls built right out into the sea, with watchtowers on their tips, and a huge length of bronze chain strung between the towers. This was to keep out invaders or unexpected visitors of any kind.

The pilot was rowed out in a small boat; the sea chain was unfastened and lowered to permit the passage of a ship's keel, and the galley from Urgoph slowly entered the harbor of Arjis Isle.

It was a trireme, actually, not a galley—a trireme with a high, castled poop and a gilded prow whose figurehead depicted a Magnate challenging the waves, brandishing in his left hand the traditional trident, and in his right a fistful of money. Yoop antlers crowned his brow.

It was all most impressive, and Dalassa was virtually bursting with pride at the way the huge ship floated with queenly

---

* And a fine motto it is! I commend it to the postal service of our own era, which is, alas, too easily "stayed" from making deliveries.

grace into her moorings and the oarbanks back-watered with perfect timing. On the quay they could hear the faint boom-boom of the drummer, setting the pace for the oarsmen, and even the crack of the overseers' whips.

Through the long slots in the trireme's side, through which the oars thrust, they glimpsed pale, woeful faces. These were the slaves chained to the oars. They looked tired and miserable and most unhappy, which is about how you might expect galley slaves to look.

Grrff peered closely at the row of sad faces, then burst into hearty guffaws. Among them he recognized several of the Soormian Priests and Deacons, including Ildth and Pervwyn, who had annoyed them earlier. He later learned that with the squashing of the Mysteriarch Ommo and the dislodging of the Talking Heads (by now all pounded into faintly sentient gravel under the righteously indignant mauls of Urgoph, save for those who had rolled off the docks of Urgoph and into the sea), the cult of the Stone Heads had disintegrated. Many of its adherents had fled north into the Desolation of Oj to become desert hermits; those who were tardy in taking flight had been pressed into Urgovian servitude. It was, all things considered, a fitting end.

The gangplank was lowered; trumpets rang; and down the gangplank came stout old Borgo Methrix himself, in all his Grand Magnatorial finery, to fold his long-lost daughter to his stately bosom.

13.

ECONOMICS OF RASCHID

Dalassa wept tears of joy, hugging her father lustily and demanding to know the current state of health enjoyed by all of her brothers, sisters and tweenies. It seemed that they were all in excellent fettle, although of course anxious as to her safety.

"May I congratulate you, Munificentessa, on this timely rescue from the gory clutches of these villainous buccaneers," murmured a suave voice from her father's side. The speaker was a slim, elegant fop adorned in lordly silks. His smile was painted on, with vermillion and mauve.

"Thank you, sir. . . ."

"Daughter, this is a visitor to our realm, Sir Gyzik, an ambassador from—" the Magnate began.

The blare of trumpets drowned out his words, however. They announced the arrival of the pirate chief and his Captains in all their ceremonial regalia. Among these was, of course, Zarcas in a flowing, open-throated white silk shirt and brown velvet knee britches. The white silk set off his tan magnificently, and Dalassa blushed as she met his eyes, which twinkled humorously. She introduced Raschid and his Captains to her father, who nodded in regal acknowledgment.

"Stand and deliver, landlubber, or, shiver me timbers but I'll be after hangin' th lot o' ye from me yardarm," said Raschid in traditional piratical fashion.

"O spare my daughter and her friends, dread corsair," said Borgo Methrix, following the approved formula, "and anything you ask shall be yours, even unto the half of my kingdom!"

"Whine an' whimper if ye will, lubber, but come across wif th' loot or I'll be after havin' yer gizzard an' tripes fer me breakfast—scuttle me fer a Jonah if'n I don'tl"

Footstools were brought out, and a folding table. The two seated themselves. A parchment was fetched, covered with skulls and crossbones and bloody crosses. Both ceremoniously signed. Then Borgo Methrix waved his silk handkerchief; Soormian slaves began to drag down to the dock kegs and casks and chests of treasure. The pirates fell upon this plunder with whoops of glee while Raschid and Borgo shook hands formally, sealing the pact.

Then everybody went back to the Residence for an early lunch. And thus were the captives ransomed.

The next day, Raschid escorted the Grand Magnate of Urgoph and his guest, Sir Gyzik, around Arjis Isle in general and the pirate town of Orgaza in particular.

Sir Gyzik was obsequious, flattering, oily, unctuous and very self-effacing. He let the Magnate and the pirate chief do all the talking. For his part, he studied the fortifications closely—without seeming to—and jotted down an occasional note on his cuff.

"Ol' Grrff don't eggzactly trust that Gyzik," announced the Karjixian Tigerman to Dalassa during a brief respite from the tour. "Who *is* he, anyway?"

"A visitor to Urgoph, my father said," murmured the blonde girl carelessly. "No one of any consequence, I'm sure."

"He sure was innerested in Cap'n Zarcas," Kurdi pointed out. "Sat nex' to him at the feast las' night, y'know? Kept peerin' at him an' starin' outa th' corner of his eye, like he almos' recognized him from somewheres. . . ."

"Yeah," growled Grrff, meditatively. "Seemed innerested in his tattoo."

"His tattoo?" repeated Dalassa, curiously. "*What* tattoo?"

"The one on his chest, just above his heart."

Dalassa pondered: now she recalled that the smooth, tanned flesh on the breast of Zarcas the Zirian indeed bore a curious heraldic design in emerald ink. She recalled having glimpsed it back aboard the *Bucket o' Blood*, during their shipboard days together.

At the time she had thought nothing about it. Now it occurred to her to wonder what it was.

That afternoon she drew fat, belligerent little Zollobus aside and asked him about it.

"Thet green tattoo on th' lad's chist?" repeated the pudgy little pirate, goggling up at her with his pop-eyes. "Why, 'tis the Royal Emblem o' th' Zirian Monarchy, lass—nuthin' else but!"

That answered her question; but it did little to solve the riddle of why Sir Gyzik should be so interested in it.

The ransom was divided, with half of the sum going to Zarcas the Zirian and his crew, the remainder being split up between the other ships which had accompanied the *Bucket* on her raiding venture, with a fixed percentage going to Raschid himself.

This was, the former prisoners learned, the way things were usually done.

While the ransom set for Dalassa, Silvermane, Grrff, Kurdi and Ishgadara had been a plump and sizable sum, neither Borgo Methrix nor the other Urgovian magnates had been discomfitted thereby.

"Took it out of the Soormian treasury," the fat Magnate grinned. The Priests had, he explained, milked the wealth of the Urgoph merchants for years; now, the cult disbanded, their treasure had been seized by the Urgovian government.

When he gloatingly described the gold bullion, the silver ingots, the sacks of pearls, rubies, sapphires, turnadots*, opals, emeralds, topazes, quanes*, amethysts, diamonds and zaraphs*, the chests of ivory, amber, ebony, malachite and jade, they were all impressed.

So, unfortunately, was Raschid the Red.

The Pirate Chief had always known the magnates of Urgoph were rolling in wealth; now he began to get some idea of just how much wealth they had to roll in. The very thought of it made his thin-lipped mouth water.

It also began to give him ideas.

Perhaps my reader should be reminded at this point that the pirates of Arjis Isle were not *exactly* criminals. They operated under charters from the legal government of Arjis Isle, which was a legitimate republic, under whose laws piracy, smuggling, buccaneering and thievery were fully lawful and even quite respectable trades.

More than just that, piracy was actually needed in order to support the economy of the Republic of Arjis. This is because

* Gems peculiar to the geology of Old Earth's last and mightiest continent. Turnadots are brownish-red gems found in matrix with sulphur and brimstone, quanes are translucent and bluish-green, believed to be fossilized water, while zaraphs are golden-colored rhinestones.

the island had no industries of its own, or very few, and supported no agriculture at all, as most of its land surface was occupied by mangrove swamps, impassable jungles, and, of course, the volcano which took up most of the center part.

A little fishing was done, and some of the jungle trees bore edible fruit; but were it not for the proceeds from the practice of piracy, the island dwellers would starve.

In a word, they theived to gain the wealth to purchase food. For the most part, they bought the food from the very islands and seaports they also robbed from. A precarious balance of economic factors had been achieved.

Nor did their victims protest too much, although they were not exactly thrilled to be raided and robbed. On the other hand, the merchants whom the pirates robbed could (and did) console themselves with the knowledge that sooner or later their stolen wealth would return to their coffers as payment for food staples.

Only Urgoph, far to the north, took no part in this peculiarly Zelphodonian exchange. Urgoph did not sell food staples; its mercantile magnates dealt in farm implements, lamp oil, lumber, spices and condiments, pearls, copra, rubber, tin, copper, zook-zook flowers, jewelry, textiles, and gazare.*

Therefore, while it did not behoove the pirates to loot and plunder and despoil the other Zelphodonian isles and realms *without restraint,* since to do so might endanger their trade relations, no such constraints held them back from the sacking of Urgoph. Which was why Zarcas the Zirian and Black Horrog had tried it in the first place.

Hitherto it had been too chancy for any but the daring Zarcas and the greedy, and stupid, Horrog. This was due to the fact that Urgoph had been virtually under the dominance of the Soormian Priests, whose supernatural powers were rightly feared by the superstitious buccaneers.

But, now that the priesthood was no more, Urgoph and its fat treasuries were fair game.

This had not escaped the notice of Raschid the Red.

True, the expedition of Zarcas had failed. But that was not due to the powers of the Soormians, but to the unexpected defense led by Silvermane and his friends. Had it not been for the stalwart Construct and his allies, the surprise raid

---

* A perfumed oil processed from the liver of sea serpents, much fancied by the ladies of fashion on the islands and archipelagoes of the Zelphodonian Sea. The oil came by overland caravans from cities along the shores of Quadquoph.

might well have succeeded. And now that the Talking Heads were gone and their priesthood dispersed, the next attack against Urgoph might well succeed—and richly.

This, by the way, had already occurred to Borgo Methrix. One of the reasons he had come in person to arrange for the freedom of his daughter and her friends was that he hoped to formulate some manner of treaty with the pirates of Arjis Isle to prevent just such an attack.

But Raschid kept him dangling. During the next week the Grand Magnate was wined and dined and shown the sights. Balls, fetes, masquerades, banquets, regattas and flower shows kept him too busy to get down to discussing business with the pirate chief. Every time he sought an audience he was put off by being asked to judge a beauty contest, give prizes in the art show arranged by the Orgaza Arts Society, lay a cornerstone, or place a wreath on the Tomb of the Unknown Buccaneer.

It was all rather frustrating.

One of the festivities, however, was of the Grand Magnate's own doing. This was the rewarding of Ganelon Silvermane, the boy Kurdi, Ishgadara the Gynosphinx and the Tigerman Grrff for their heroic part in the successful defense of Urgoph against the pirate raid. They were all created Honorary Magnates Third Class.

Silvermane accepted the honor moodily. He would have liked to get going: the longer they stayed here on Arjis Isle, the less happy he was. He was only too aware that Black Horrog had it in for them, and that Raschid the Red was very friendly with Horrog, and that something was brewing.

He suspected treachery of some sort, he wasn't sure what.

And, as things turned out, he was only too right.

When the time came at last for them to depart, everybody but Borgo Methrix was delighted at the prospect. The portly Grand Magnate had not been able to arrange a treaty with Raschid. The wily pirate chief had listened sympathetically to his arguments, but had put him off with evasive words and half-promises.

Sir Gyzik, on the other hand, seemed only too pleased at the prospect of disembarking from Arjis Isle. His ill-concealed pleasure puzzled them all. Particularly Kurdi.

"Maybe it's got somethin' to do with that message he sent the other day," muttered the youth, half to himself.

"Huh?" grunted Grrff. "What message izzat, cub?"

"I dunno," the boy shrugged. "But . . . y'know that bird

with th' talary* plumage ol' Gyzik fussed over so much—th' one he kep' in th' li'l wicker cage?"

"Yeah. . . ?"

"Well, t'other day I was goin' by his room an' I seed him—"

"*Saw* him," corrected Grrff absently.

"—I saw him tie a piece o' paper around ol' bird's leg and letum fly away home," Kurdi finished.

Grrff scratched his muzzle with one wicked claw.

"Hmm. Well, Gyzik is some sorta *ambassador* er something, so it wuz prob'ly a whatchacallit, *you* know, diplomatic message," rumbled Grrff.

"Guess so," said the youth. "Still, it *is* queer."

"So it is," nodded the Tigerman.

"Wonder where 'home' is t' Gyzik," added the boy. The furry Karjixian shrugged one burly shoulder.

"Dunno. Le's go eat."

At dinner that night—a farewell feast Raschid was giving in Borgo Methrix' honor—it occurred to Grrff to inquire on that point of Borgo Methrix himself. He had been seated on the left, right next to the Grand Magnate.

"What's that, my dear chap? Sir Gyzik? Why, I thought I had explained all that when I first arrived on this delightful island," purred Borgo Methrix casually. "Sir Gyzik is an ambassador from the eastern realm of Ziria, recently sent to our court to inquire after a missing prince left over from the former dynasty. Seems that King Urzang the Usurper is anxious to discover the whereabouts of this missing princeling, one Zarcas, son of the late King Zaractacas . . . odd, now that I think of it! Why, the missing Zirian prince has the same name as Captain Zarcas, the pirate who carried all of you dear people off after the raid on Urgoph. . . ."

"*Odd* ain't eggzactly the word fer it," groaned the Tigerman, with a sinking feeling in the region of his stomach.

Suddenly, he had a hunch about what had been in the note Sir Gyzik had attached to the bird's leg just before setting it free to fly back home.

And now he knew that "home" was the Kingdom of Ziria, from which Vlasko and Zollobus had fled with the young

---

* A color unique to the octave of visible light in the age of Ganelon Silvermane, next to purple. In our day talary was invisible, being in the ultra-violet. The spectrum has broadened a bit in the seven hundred million years between our epoch and the Eon of the Falling Moon, and several colors invisible to us at both ends of the visible light octave can clearly be seen by the Gondwanians.

prince into exile, to escape the murderous attentions of the Usurper.

"Do have some more of this Kakkawakka stew, my boy," said Borgo Methrix. "Really quite delicious cuisine!"

"Thanks, but ol' Grrff jus' lost his appetite," growled the Karjixian, worriedly.

One item of bad news is enough to ruin the finest feast, or so runs the old Karjixian proverb. Alas, this feast was to be spoiled by two unhappy discoveries.

For after the feast, Borgo Methrix was arrested and taken into the personal custody of Raschid the Red. He was being held to ransom!

"But my father just *paid* the ransom," stormed Dalassa.

"Quite right, dear lady," grinned the Pirate Chief. "But that was *your* ransom—yours and your friends'. And you are free to go. Your father, however, is quite another case: as reigning Grand Magnate of Urgoph, his ransom is . . . the entire contents of the Urgovian treasury! Come, I have all my terms written up in this little document, which I hope you will deliver to the Magnatorial Council upon your swift return to Urgoph. Indeed," he laughed; "if you deliver my demands, 'twill save me the cost of seamail!"

Raschid could be most economical at times.

14.

GANELON SILVERMANE DECIDES

The next morning our friends gathered in the apartments which Vlasko and Zollobus maintained on the second story of the inn Jolly Roger. Their hosts were absent, and this gave them the privacy they needed to discuss the recent, unhappy turn of events.

Ganelon felt miserable and gloomy that Borgo Methrix should have gotten himself into such trouble while doing his best to extricate them from exactly the same sort of predicament.

Dalassa was seething with fury over the treachery of Raschid, and filled with determination to set her father free somehow.

Of them all, only the Karjixian Tigerman was philosophical about the situation. "Ol' Raschid," he opined wisely, "he's a cunning rascal, the sort ya can only trust as far as ya can throw 'im. He's as twisty and slick as a snake. Gotta . *expect* him to do ya dirty, if he possibly can."

"But my father entered Orgaza harbor under a flag of truce-and-parley," stormed the blonde girl, striding up and down like a caged tigress.

Grrff merely shrugged. Ganelon sat on the window seat, cracking his knuckles moodily, looking somber and unhappy. Kurdi perched on a three-legged stoool, kicking his heels and looking pertly from one to the other expectantly. Ishgadara lay stretched out before a roaring fire, grooming her tummy with a huge pink tongue.

"Well, one thing at least is certain," said Ganelon after a

while. "We can't just up anchor and let your father's ship sail us back to Urgoph, leaving the Magnate behind in chains. He's in this predicament because of us, so it's up to us to get him out of it. Somehow. . . ."

"How?" demanded Dalassa, bluntly.

Silvermane avoided her eye. "I don't know," he confessed in slow tones.

After a while, he spoke up again. "On the other hand, I don't see what we could do to get your father out. . . . We certainly can't take on the whole pirate kingdom in a fight, just the five of us. That wouldn't be a fight, that'd be a massacre. And we'd be the ones getting massacred. And once it was over, your father would still be a prisoner. . . ."

Dalassa said nothing, but glowered mutinously, sulking.

"So we can't just go, and we can't stay an' fight, izzat it, big man?" inquired Grrff with grim humor. "Kinda in a pickle, ain't we?"

"We are," admitted Silvermane gloomily.

"Whyn't we do *both*, then?" chirped Kurdi brightly. They looked at him askance. The boy jumped off the stool.

"Le's sail outa sight, like as if we wuz goin' off to Urgoph," the youth explained, "then, onc't we're outa range, come flyin' back on Ishy and bust inta th' jail!"

"Ishy can't fly, they trimmed her feathers," Grrff pointed out.

"Feathers growingk pack by now," rumbled the Gynosphinx, lazily licking the fur on her hind legs. They looked at one another in growing excitement.

"We c'd come back by night," mused Grrff, "land ona palace *roof*—"

"Break in through a *skylight* or sumphin—" Kurdi chirped eagerly.

"Cut our way in to father's *cell*," said Dalassa, eyes sparkling, "and be off before anybody knows what's happened—"

Ganelon thought it over somberly. Then the gloomy expression vanished from his features. His eyes flashed, his shoulders straightened. He had reached a decision.

"It's worth a try," he announced.

They must await the morning tide before setting sail, so the rest of that day was spent in making ready for the venture.

Dalassa went down to the docks to apprise the captain of her father's ship of their imminent departure. He swore to have everything shipshape by dawn, and sent his officers out to comb the waterfront dives for his seamen, who were hap-

pily boozing, gambling and wenching in the immemorial fashion of sailors ashore in every land and age.

Grrff went marching off to the Residence to inform the
Pirate Chief they were leaving. Raschid was delighted and
promised to have his scribes draw up the new ransom demands and deliver them to the docks by dawn.

Ganelon and Kurdi took Ishgadara for a walk along the
beach, and, once they were out of the sight of any spying
eyes from town, let her practice flying—first on her own, and
then with the two of them as passengers—to make certain
that she was airworthy once again. She was a little wobbly in
the air, but it didn't seem likely that it would matter.

They got together that evening and packed up their gear,
said their good-byes to Vlasko and Zollobus, and went down
to the Urgovian ship to store their belongings away and explain their plans to the captain. They would have dinner on
board that night so as to be able to leave first thing in the
morning, with the tide.

In the rush of last-minute preparations, they didn't have a
chance to say farewell to Zarcas the Zirian. When they
remembered they had not paid him their respects, it was too
late to do anything about it.

Also, they remembered a trifle guiltily, they had neglected
to inform him that Sir Gyzik was a Zirian spy and had discovered his secret identity. This was considerably more
serious than just forgetting to say good-bye to him; but there
wasn't much they could do about it.

"We can always give him the news by seamail, once we are
back in Urgoph," Ganelon reminded them. "First things first:
let's help Borgo Methrix escape, and worry about Captain
Zarcas later on."

Night fell. They slept in their bunks. With dawn, the *Pride
of Urgoph* weighed anchor and drifted out on the tides. Once
out to sea, the Soormian galley slaves groaned and bent to
their tasks, unhappily dreaming of jollier times back in the
service of the Holy Heads. Arjis Isle dwindled in the distance
across the green and shining sea, fading at last from sight.

All that day they sailed north in the direction of Urgoph.

Only one little thing disturbed them. That was that Sir
Gyzik had not shown up at dawn to debark with them as
planned. Scuttlebutt on the docks had it that the Zirian ambassador had chartered a fast schooner and had departed
around midnight, bound for an unknown destination.

"Ziria, *I* bet!" said Kurdi in positive tones.

"I suppose you're right," sighed Ganelon heavily. "He

probably can't wait to get back home and reap the glory for
having located the lost prince . . ."

"The glory—or the reward?" murmured the Tigerman,
cynically.

"I wish we had been able to tell Zarcas—*Captain* Zarcas, I
mean—about what we discovered," complained Dalassa.

"One thing at a time," said Silvermane.

"Hmph!"

By nightfall they were many leagues out to sea, well beyond the reach of any piratical reprisals. (So they hoped,
anyway.) During the twenty-four days they had resided on
Arjis Isle, they had gained a healthy respect for the corsairs
as masters of sea warfare. An unarmed merchantman could
do little if attacked by the lean, swift, deadly pirate crafts.
With any luck, though, this would not happen.

Kurdi regretted most not being able to say good-bye to
Zork Aargh. But the lovable little mechanoid had been absent
from his accustomed haunts during their last day in Orgaza
when the boy had gone looking for him.

In the nine weeks that had passed since they discovered
him on Korscio, the gypsy youth and the comical little robot
had become fast friends and playmates. Kurdi knew that he
would miss his mechanical pal.

Night fell, and the Falling Moon rose, flooding the sparkling sea with its brilliance. Ganelon and Grrff climbed
astride Ishgadara's broad and furry back, and she rapidly ascended into the air. Both Kurdi and Dalassa had loudly
claimed a share of this adventure, but to their vociferous
pleas Silvermane had turned a deaf ear.

"Ishgadara's wing-tip feathers have only just grown back,"
he said firmly. "She's not quite up to carrying so much
weight. And Borgo Methrix is not a small man, or a light
burden. If we load Ishy up with all of us she may not be able
to get back to the *Pride of Urgoph* with his additional
weight."

They didn't like being left behind, but there wasn't much
they could say to that. So they watched, unhappily, as the
sphinx girl flew across the shining face of the Falling Moon
and dwindled into the distance.

The ship rode at sea anchor, bobbing up and down with
the waves. Occasionally an inquisitive Merperson would poke
his or her spiny-crested head up out of the water to see if
they were all right and to find out why they were pausing
here.

An hour passed. So did another.

"Surely, they should have been back by now," muttered Dalassa, huddled in a warm wool cloak, clinging to the rail.

"I dunno," said Kurdi. "Maybe they ran inta *trouble*."

Dalassa said nothing, but she bit her lip and strained her eyes, peering over the silvery waves.

By dawn the rescuers still had not returned. Something very definitely had gone wrong with the plan.

"Maybe they got captured," sighed Kurdi worriedly.

"Perhaps the flying creature could not return with the added weight of the Magnate your father, Munificentessa," murmured the captain, whose name was Remix Drogatha and who was stoutly built himself and red of face.

"Or possibly they are experiencing difficulty in locating the *Pride of Urgoph*, a tiny speck amidst the waters of the main," suggested one of the Urgovian dignitaries who had accompanied the Grand Magnate on the expedition to Arjis.

"What shall we do, Munificentessa?" asked the captain.

"We'll wait," said Dalassa.

And wait they did, all that day and the following night.

By the next morning they simply could wait no longer, but must proceed north across the Zelphodon to Urgoph.

It was a matter of grim necessity: the *Pride of Urgoph* did not carry sufficient supplies of fresh water for a sustained sea journey.

Whatever had become of Ganelon Silvermane and Grrff the Xombolian and Ishgadara the Gynosphinx—to say nothing of the Grand Magnate Borgo Methrix—the Urgovian merchantman could linger in these waters no longer.

However reluctantly, Captain Drogatha commanded that the sea anchor be taken aboard and the sails trimmed. The drums took up the beat and the Soormian slaves bent again to their oars, having heartily enjoyed the day-long respite from their toils.

By mid-morn they were progressing at a steady pace into the northern waters, riding before a brisk and spanking breeze.

Then the alarm was given. An alert Urgovian, perched high in the crow's nest, sang out to those on deck a cry guaranteed to stir the pulse of any seaman:

"*Sails ho!*"

"Where away?" demanded Remix Drogatha, through a paper trumpet.

"South-away, Cap'n!"

"How many?"

"Two, it be. No, three!"

"Can you read their colors, my man?"

A breathless, aching silence, while all strained their eyes to the south across the shining waves.

"Aye, Captain," came the answer from aloft. " . . . *they fly the bloody flag."*

"Pirates," said Remix Drogatha heavily. "Pirates!"

Dalassa had taken to her cabin with a sick headache when the time came to up anchor and sail off home. Now she had come on deck to discover the cause of all the commotion. Hurriedly wrapping a cloak about her lissom form—like all Urgovian ladies of genteel birth, she slept in the raw—she joined the captain at the wheel. Kurdi came scampering at her heels.

"What is happening, Captain Drogatha?" she demanded.

"We are being pursued by three buccaneers, Munificentessa," that stout personage informed her.

"From Arjis Isle?" she inquired breathlessly.

"I cannot say, Munificentessa."

"Can we outrun them?"

"I certainly *hope* so, Munificentessa."

"One of 'em's the *Bucket o' Blood*," said Kurdi excitedly, peering out to sea. Dalassa looked outraged. It was, indeed, a bit much—to be captured twice by the same pirate ship.

"Well, for goodness sake, *try* to outrun them, captain!"

"I'll do my best," the captain muttered, chewing on his mustache. "We have a head start on the rogues, but they have ships much slimmer and lighter and swifter than ours. Well, we shall give the rascals a race for their money, at any rate—"

And he stomped out with a rolling gait, solemnly booming out orders through his paper trumpet.

For four hours they led the pirate flotilla a merry chase. But from the very beginning it was a chase with a foregone conclusion. There was simply no way the heavily built merchant ship, broad in the beam to accommodate her capacious hold, and riding low in the water, could forever outdistance the slim, lean rakish wolves of the sea.

By early afternoon they surrendered.

There was nothing else the Urgovians could do. Sailing from Urgoph under flag-of-truce, they had of course shipped no fighting men in the crew. It was either a matter of surrender and be spared, or fight it out and be boarded and, probably, slaughtered to the last man.

So Captain Drogatha surrendered.

Zarcas and Squint came aboard to accept the captain's sword and to disarm the crew. Squint grinned and waved at Dalassa and the boy, but Zarcas, flushing guiltily, tried to avoid her eye. For her part, the blonde girl ignored his very existence.

They were taken aboard the *Bucket o' Blood* again, while Zarcas left a prize crew aboard the *Pride of Urgoph* to sail the merchantman back to Arjis Isle. When he regained his own deck, he determinedly sought out Dalassa to explain things, although from the distinctly uncomfortable expression on his face it was blatantly obvious that he would rather not have had to confront her under these circumstances.

"M'lady . . . the *Bucket* and these two other ships were offshore on sentry cruise, when word came from the Captain's Council to sail north and apprehend the *Pride of Urgoph* . . . seems two from your company, on Ishgadara (and I can guess which two!) attempted a flying raid on the Residence, but were captured trying the rescue the Grand Magnate . . . I—I'm sorry, girl!"

He stammered out his explanation lamely, then flushed and went silent. For she walked by him as if he did not exist, and vanished below. His brow thunderous, tight-lipped with rage, he stormed off to pace his quarterdeck. No one dared speak to or look at him: all knew how he felt toward the Urgovian princess.

Zork Aargh came timidly up to where Kurdi stood, forlorn and rather miserable, caught in the riptide of these adult emotions he could scarcely comprehend.

"Self is hoping still to be friends with small human person," piped the little mechanoid shyly.

Lurdi Kurdi flung his arms about the bulbous metal body and hugged it fiercely.

"Oh, Zorky, *ever'*thing's gone wrong!" he wailed.

And so it had.

15.

ISHGADARA GETS IMPATIENT

During the day and the night it took the pirate flotilla and its captives to sail back into the southern seas to Arjis Isle, Dalassa and Kurdi learned little more concerning the fate of Grrff and Ganelon and Ishgadara.

They still did not know how it was that the three of them—very formidable warriors, all—had come to be captured. But at least they were still alive and apparently uninjured, as was the Magnate Borgo Methrix. This afforded some consolation to Kurdi and Dalassa; but the failure of their plans ruined everything. And now they were prisoners again!

Near sunset on the day after their recapture, they hove to in the harbor of Arjis Isle and the ships were made fast to one of the docks. Under ostensibly heavy guard, the prisoners were escorted to the Residence, were served a good dinner, and were locked away in separate cells.

It was depressing to find themselves back in the same town they had sailed out of five days before. They passed a restless night, wondering how they could possibly extricate themselves from their situation.

The next morning, in the exercise yard, they encountered their friends. An enlightened despot, Raschid well knew that prisoners mewed up in lightless cells languish and sicken. And it is never wise to risk the health of people you are holding for ransom. So daily his prisoners were allowed out in the exercise yard and were permitted to stroll about, enjoying the sunshine and the open air under the watchful eye of vigilant guards.

And there were Ganelon Silvermane and Grrff the Xombolian and Ishgadara (with her wings clipped again) and Borgo Methrix. Their reunion was noisy and tearful, with many back-slappings and hugs and plenty of kisses.

"All ready an' *waitin'* fer us, they wuz," growled the Tigerman after giving Kurdi a rib-cracking embrace. "Musta knowed what we wuz up to."

"They felled us with *flowers*, of all things," explained Silvermane somberly. "Resembled orchids, but their perfume was essentially narcotic and put us to sleep before we realized what was happening."

"Thought *sumphin* wuz funny, all they flower pots an' windy-boxes ina a hall outsida yer dad's cell," grumbled Grrff. "Ol' Grrff sez it wuz pretty scrumptious fer a dungeon, but big man here, he didn't give it no mind. . . ."

Ganelon grinned sheepishly, but said nothing.

"Have you heard if Urgoph has yet replied to that red rascal's exorbitant demand for my ransom, daughter?" inquired Borgo Methrix worriedly. It had probably occurred to him, as it had also occurred to them, that Urgoph might well decide the demands were too high and simply refuse to pay them. After all, even Grand Magnates were expendable. All the town had to do was elect another in Borgo's place. Dalassa admitted that she had heard nothing on this point either one way or the other. But she doubted that Urgoph had yet replied, as the ship bearing the message had been captured, and she did not know if Raschid the Red had sent duplicate demands by seamail. Probably, Urgoph had not even heard that its chief executive was being held for ransom on the pirate isle, and thus had yet to decide the question of whether to ransom him back or replace him with another, less expensive magistrate.

For the next three days the captives languished in their solitary cells, mingling together only briefly in the exercise yard. They were under such strict surveillance that it was not possible for them to discuss the possibilities of making an escape.

Lacking the company of his friends, Kurdi moped. The lively, likable boy missed Ganelon and the others and severely suffered from being deprived of their companionship. His only solace was Zork Aargh.

The bulbous little mechanoid had been assigned to guard duties in the Residence for a week. This was commonly the practice on Arjis Isle, for the Captains—each jealous and sus-

picious of the other, and all with a wary eye on Raschid—
had long ago agreed their crews should share police duties in
the town and the palace so that none of them could build a
power base stronger or more loyal than the other, especially
not Raschid.

Zork played checkers with Kurdi and did his level best to
cheer the boy up. He conveyed messages from Ganelon and
Grrff and Dalassa, and was a source of amusement and gos-
sip to Kurdi. The little gypsy boy, an orphan, had never really had a playmate before; and the robot had never really had
a friend. They became inseparable in less time than it takes
me to say so.

The brief messages conveyed back and forth between the
prisoners by the helpful little mechanoid often contained surreptitious references to plans for escape. It is difficult to ar-
rive at much of a decision when all you can do is scribble a
few words on a bit of paper—then wait a day or so for a reply.

Luckily, Zork Aargh could not read, so his own loyalties
were not compromised. Anyway, they were divided, those
loyalties. He confided to Kurdi on more than one occasion
that Zarcas the Zirian was distinctly unhappy at their im-
prisonment: since their ransom had already been paid, it was
the opinion of the Prince of Ziria that their recapture, reim-
prisonment and reransom were strictly contrary to the ethical
system observed by the pirates of Zelphodon, an unwritten
law known as "The Code o' the Sea."

But there was little he could do to alter or affect
circumstances.

In answer to worried and repeated questions from Borgo
Methrix, Zorky asked about and discovered that Raschid had
indeed dispatched his new ransom demands to the city fathers
of Urgoph via an obliging Merperson. If it took as long to
get a reply this time as it had taken the time before, then
they could expect to cool their heels in their cells for another
week, at least.

But, as things turned out, this did not prove necessary.

For on the evening of the sixth day after Kurdi and
Dalassa were brought back to Arjis Isle, Ishgadara took
matters into her own hands. Or paws, to be precise.

The Gynosphinx, like most other four-footed creatures,
heartily disliked being penned up behind steel bars and stone
walls. Part of her was lion, and lions have never enjoyed
zoos any more than canaries enjoy cages. So, after being

patient for as long as she could stand to be, the big sphinx girl decided to bust loose and free her friends. She couldn't fly yet, but she could do plenty of fighting. And *this* time she intended to steer clear of all flower pots and window boxes.

The occasion she chose for her escape was right in the middle of a Timely Interruption. Noisy diversions are probably the best times to pick for jailbreaks—if you can manage it. And in that respect, Ishgadara was lucky.

For, quite suddenly, the Residence of the pirate chief was in an uproar. The halls and stairways were crowded with running, cursing, shouting figures, and everything was in turmoil and confusion. The time seemed to Ishgadara most opportune for breaking out. It seemed to the huge, determined creature that they could most likely escape while everybody in the palace was too busy and too alarmed to worry about a few fleeing prisoners.

So the Gynosphinx rose to her full height, which was considerable, and gave the cell door a push. Hinges squealed and bolts screeched, but the door held. Becoming impatient with the silly thing, she battered the walls which held the hinges, striking with her great paws and with all of the enormous strength of her forearms and back and burly shoulders.

The walls were of solid stone and well-mortared: but it takes a lot more than stone blocks and mortar to keep an infuriated Gynosphinx penned up. The mortar crumbled, spewing chips and splattering gray gritty dust across the corridor. A block of stone loosened; then another. One more biff of her huge paws dislodged them, and the wall wherein the doorframe was set began to crumble and came apart.

She seized the tottering door in her claws and wrenched it loose. It fell into the corridor with an enormous clang and clatter, and Ishy was free.

Poor little Zork Aargh, who was on dungeon guard that night, came whirring down the hall, windmilling his several arms, piping timid protests.

"Begging pardon, but is forbidden to escape! Is definitely against rules and regulations," he complained tinnily. Ishy, now thoroughly aroused and quite enjoying herself, was about to bat the little mechanoid aside, but thought better of it. She picked him up and tucked him under her arm. He kicked and squirmed but was quite powerless to free himself.

Waddling down the hall on her hind legs, she came to Ganelon's door and beat the wall in, ripped the barred door out of its frame and set him free. Then the two of them freed Grrff in a similar manner. Before the world was half an hour older, Dalassa, Kurdi and Borgo Methrix were likewise free of Durance Vile.

Prowling about, they found their gear and weapons stacked in a storeroom, and soon accoutered themselves. Whirling his ygdraxel with the gleam of vengeance in his eye, the Karjixian Tigerman felt ready for anything.

"Now how d'we git outa here?" he demanded.

"Is forbidden," moaned Zork Aargh from Ishgadara's armpit.

"What'll we do with him, knock him apart for scrap?" inquired Grrff. Kurdi hurriedly sprang to his friend's defense.

"Zorky won't give no alarm, you leavum alone!" said the boy stoutly.

Ganelon did not know how to silence the mechanoid without destroying him, and liked the little robot too much to be guilty of *that.*

"I suggest we bring him along with us," he advised. Ishgadara grinned, tucked the whimpering metal man more firmly under her arm, and waddled along, leading the way. Before long they encountered another cell-block wherein were pent the crew and officers of the *Pride of Urgoph,* who hailed them spiritedly.

Squint was guarding this block of cells. One glimpse at the determined host which approached him grimly, bristling with weapons, and the skinny pointy-nosed yellow-skinned Ikzikian hastily surrendered. They used his keys to unlock the cells, which was a lot quicker than letting Ishy bash them in. They had to bring Squint along with them, too.

They reached the stairway which led up to the ground floor of the edifice, collecting One-Eye as they went. Up the stairs they hurried, by now an armed band comprised of considerable numbers. They were determined not to be recaptured again, and were quite ready to fight.

"What's all the ruckus about, anyway?" huffed Grrff, loping up the stairs, to Squint.

"Gut me fer a flounder, matey, but I've no idee," wheezed Zarcas' first mate anxiously.

"Do you know what's going on, One-Eye?" inquired Silvermane.

"Danged if'n I do," swore the pirate. "Hit *dew* sound important, though! War, revvylushun er mutiny, *I* say—"

Zarcas, serving that night as captain of the guard, met them at the front entrance with a drawn sword. One glance at the mob told him the wisest thing to do would be to surrender. He proffered his sword to Ganelon Silvermane with a quiet smile.

"Discretion being, as ever, the better part of valor, sir, I shall not stand in your way," he murmured.

"What's going on down in the city?" asked Silvermane distractedly. The Zirian shrugged nonchalantly.

"I think we are being attacked," he drawled casually. "But from whence, or by whom, I've no idea. My sword, Sir Silvermane—"

"Keep it. You'll probably need it," said the Construct.

"Docks be thet-away," hinted Squint with a wink. He was not altogether unhappy that the adventurers were escaping.

"Yes, that's the quickest way," Ganelon nodded. Then, to the Zirian: "I'm afraid you'll have to come with us."

"It will be my pleasure," grinned the pirate captain. Whether it was war, riot, insurrection or invasion, the safest place in all of Orgaza was probably directly behind Ganelon Silvermane and Grrff the Xombolian.

They made their way through the dark streets with no one even noticing. Everyone was running around waving torches or cutlasses and yelling his head off. Nobody seemed to have any notion of what was happening at all.

Dalassa, who had squirmed her way through the throng to a place beside Zarcas, now uttered a decidedly unladylike snort of derision. The captain elevated one brow ironically.

"What amuses you, m'lady?"

The girl eyed him frostily, a glint of mischief in her gaze.

"Oh, nothing . . . I was just thinking . . . you've captured us twice, and now we've captured you. I think we have one more capture coming to us, is all!"

Zarcas smiled at her jest, but his eyes were serious. In the light of flickering torches, a smudge on her adorable nose, her bright hair loose and tousled, she looked irresistibly beautiful.

"If that amuses you, m'lady," he said softly, "then laugh yet more. For if 'tis conquest that pleases your fancy, the score is even, though you know it not."

"Eh?" said Dalassa, puzzled. He smiled crookedly.

"You took my heart a captive, lady, long ago," said Zarcas the Zirian.

Dalassa crimsoned and dropped her eyes. When she raised them to meet his again, they were brimming with tears. He said nothing, nor did she. But he shifted his sword into his other hand, and took her hand in his free one. And they went on together through the noisy, busy streets of Orgaza hand in hand.

Noticing this byplay, Grrff grinned hugely and nudged Silvermane in the ribs, calling his attention to the twain. The giant smiled, but his heart was empty. A synthetic creation, not even remotely human, he knew that he could never love, for he was the only one of his breed alive in all of Gondwane in this age. And the knowledge made him sad.

Not that he knew much about love, of course.

They came down to the docks without adventure or mishap, and there it was they discovered what had aroused the turmoil.

Squint stopped short, gaping incredulously.

"Shiver me timbers," he snorted unbelievingly, "but we're after bein' *invaded*—!"

And so they were: a huge armada of sailing ships was arrayed at the mouth of the harbor, held at bay for the moment by the mighty chain which stretched between the two watchtowers and blocked the entrance. There were thirty-two ships in all, and they fairly bristled with well-armed fighting men.

"So we be, by Neddy Dingo!" swore One-Eye. "But who or whut dew be invadin' o' us?"

They strained their eyes through the murk to mark the flags which fluttered from the mastheads.

Then Zarcas turned pale and his grip on Dalassa's hand tightened.

"It is Ziria come at last," he said heavily. "Just as I always feared. . . ."

"Ol' Grrff hopes that sneak, Gyzik, got a good price," the Tigerman growled, his furry nap bristling. " 'Cause Grrff'd like t' stuff it down his gullet, coin by coin!"

But more than grim words were needed now. For the invasion from Ziria was well underway, and they were caught smack in the middle of it.

Book Four

THE GREAT ZIRIAN INVASION

The Scene: Orgaza on Arjis Isle; The High Seas; The Kakkawakka Islands.

New Characters: Duke Calaphron, Baron Fraxas, Count Wuffram, and Other Zirians; Several Hundred Kakkawakka Islanders, and Two Old Friends.

16.
RESOLVING THE DILEMMA

On the docks, Zarcas encountered his fellow captains, Vlasko and Zollobus. The two were fuming with impatience to come to grips with the Zirian invaders. But they couldn't—and here lay the irony of Orgaza's defense system. For, while the sea chain which blocked the narrow entrance to the harbor certainly performed its function in keeping the invaders *out*, it also kept the defenders *in*.

In terse, rapid words Zarcas explained the problem to Ganelon and his companions. With the harbor mouth blocked by the huge chain, the invading ships could not enter the harbor to attempt a landing in force. But neither could the pirate ships get out to fight them off. It was a peculiar sort of stalemate.

"But didn't you envision this problem when the defense system was originally devised?" asked Silvermane. Captain Zarcas shrugged disparagingly.

"We've never been invaded before, you know," he said lamely. And he muttered something about the uniquely lawful status of the pirates of Arjis Isle. Silvermane nodded, looking baffled.

"Them Zirians is gonna land up th' coast and hit you from overland," growled Grrff the Xombolian warningly.

"Probably," sighed Zarcas. "But there isn't much we can do about that."

"There *are* some ships out there, embattled with the Zirians, you know," said Dalassa, straining her eyes through the murk. And indeed, three lean-prowed galleys, flying the bloody flag of Arjis, were entangled with the Zirians. Pirates

131

had closed and boarded a couple of the Zirian ships, and were even now swarming aboard, waving their cutlasses and yelling.

"I know, we maintain night patrols against just such an eventuality," murmured Zarcas. "Who has patrol duty this week, Squint?"

The lemon-yellow Ikzikian mused, fingering his jaw.

"Hit be ol' Scrimshaw, I think, Capting. Him and Baba th' Barbarous got night duty." He named the third and the sixth in the piratical hierarchy. Zarcas nodded gloomily.

"Well, there goes Scrimshaw, poor devil," he groaned. Two of the Zirians had closed with Scrimshaw's ship, bombarding it with Heek Fire. Already the upper works were blazing.

By dawn the Zirians had disposed of Baba as well, and the pirate patrol was no more. The stalemate was still in effect, and pirates now thronged the two curving walls of stone that enclosed the green harbor like twin arms embracing an immense emerald. The Zirians made frequent sallies against them, but for each pirate they slew half a dozen took his place.

"Wargo has charge of the wall, I see," murmured Zarcas, shading his eyes. Vlasko and Zollobus were chafing at the bit.

"Must be *some* way we kin git our ships out thar," griped the dour old salt to his fat friend.

"But *how?*" groaned Zollobus.

The escaped captives had gone aboard the *Bucket o' Blood*, all except for the Urgovian dignitaries and their crew, who had returned to their own ship, the *Pride of Urgoph*. Since dawn they had lain low, not wishing to be recaptured again. Fortunately for their peace of mind, Raschid the Red had too many other things to worry about to even be bothered by news of the jailbreak.

The pirate chief had established his command post atop a saloon which fronted on the harbor of Arjis Isle, and whose second-story windows afforded him and his staff a clear and uninterrupted view of the scene of the hostilities. He was in a frothing fury, was Raschid, and no wonder.

By noon the Zirians attacked the sea wall and cut down its defenders to the last corsair.

By three in the afternoon the wall had been successfully re-captured by a daring raid led from two different directions by Black Horrog and Zarcas the Zirian.

By late afternoon the stalemate continued. But now it could be seen that the Zirian fleet was becoming bored and restive as were the pirates. For squadrons of their ships, detaching themselves from the main body of the fleet, went cruising off, one squadron sailing east along the coast, the other sailing west. The enemy ships soon vanished from sight, but it was blatantly obvious that the invaders were going to attempt an attack on the pirates' town from overland, even as that old campaigner Grrff the Xombolian had predicted the evening before.

Raschid organized two war parties and sent them off into the jungles to either side of the town, hoping to waylay the Zirians. Since two of his captains, Zarcas and Horrog, were still holding the wall, he placed Vlasko and Zollobus in charge of the land parties.

Since Wargo had fallen that morning in defense of the wall, it could be seen that the pirate chief was rapidly running out of Captains.

"If only some diversion would occur, forcing the Zirians to withdraw from the harbor mouth, we could sail out to encounter them on the high seas," he said grimly. Even in the best of times, Raschid did not enjoy being frustrated, and patience was not among the few virtues he possessed.

By nightfall, Vlasko and Zollobus returned to Orgaza in weary triumph, having succeeded in ambushing the Zirian war parties and in slaughtering them to the last man. Or nearly so, at any rate.

For they had taken one of the Zirians prisoner, having recognized him in the moonlight.

It was Sir Gyzik, the sly and treacherous Zirian ambassador and master spy. The oily tattletale was a trifle the worse for wear, but, other than a lump on his brow and the fact that he had been run through the shoulder by Vlasko's rapier, he was relatively unharmed.

He was, however, furious.

"I demand that Your Excellency observe and respect my diplomatic immunity," he declared frostily. "As an open and avowed envoy of the Majesty of Ziria, it is an affront to international law to abuse an envoy plenipotentiary—"

Raschid made a rude sound with his thin lips. "Simmer down, me bucko, or I'll hoist yer 'diplomatic immunity' from me yardarm!" he retorted in traditional piratical fashion. "You bloody Zirians are breaking international law by this unprovoked invasion of a friendly island, so don't go preaching your high-and-mighty law to me."

"Nonsense," snapped Gyzik. "It is you repulsive corsairs who have created the breach in the first place, by knowingly giving refuge and a high place in your Council to a Zirian outlaw for whom my royal master has searched these ten years. . . . I refer to your own Captain Zarcas."

Raschid looked thunderstruck. His eyes bulged and his jaw dropped. He regarded the captive incredulously.

"Zarcas?" he repeated, mystified. "Why in the name of little green fishes do you want *Zarcas?*"

Bending nearer, Sir Gyzik told him.

A gleam of unholy glee shone in the eyes of the pirate chief. He would have been happy to have gotten rid of Zarcas the Zirian long ago, for he envied the dashing young buccaneer his success, his seamanship, and his popularity with the other pirates. Regarding the young Captain with wary suspicion as a potential rival, he had long desired to rid himself of the *Bucket o' Blood* and her handsome and gallant master. And now the solution to his old dilemma, as well as an easy way out of the present problem, had dropped into his lap.

"Bring me Captain Zarcas," he commanded one of the guards.

Zarcas, however, was nowhere to be found. He and Horrog had been relieved by two lesser Captains, Gronk and Illibus, who had taken their places on the wall. Horrog had gone to the nearest grog shop, which was remaining open all night during this period of national emergency to solace the thirsts of the stalwart defenders, and Zarcas was nowhere about. At least, he was not aboard the *Bucket o' Blood,* where one might reasonably have expected to find him.

This was because Zarcas and Grrff and Ganelon Silvermane had gone off together to try out an idea that had occurred to the Construct.

One way to break the siege of Orgaza would be to create a diversion, obviously. An attack from the air would perhaps be enough to divert the Zirians from the stalemate. And Ishgadara was, of course, always willing to enjoy a good fight, as well as a flight.

The major difficulty blocking this plan was that she could no longer fly, for the long feathers which adorned the tips of her wings had been clipped at the command of Raschid the Red. But Ganelon had wondered if it might not be possible to tie *artificial feathers* to the ends of her wings, holding them on with straps and cords. The Gynosphinx was extremely dubious as to whether or not this would work, but cheerfully agreed to give it a try.

Stiff palm-fronds, which were about the size of her wingtip feathers, had been tied in place, rigged with cords and straps. Ascending to the air, the sphinx-girl swooped about in wobbly circles for a bit, descending to report that all was well.

"Me no flyingk fery far," she announced, "and no goingk fery high, but me gettum there hokay."

"Very well, Sir Silvermane," said Zarcas, "we can fly on the back of this obliging lady as far as the Zirian fleet—but what then? Landing two or three warriors in the midst of the Zirian navy is not likely to create all that much of a diversion."

"I don't plan to land," said Ganelon.

"Well, then, what do you intend to do?" murmured Zarcas sardonically. "Drop stones on their heads, is that it?"

"Exactly that," Silvermane acknowledged. "But very special stones. . . ."

Zarcas was mystified. But no less so than the Zirians themselves, about half an hour later, when the first of their ships exploded into flame. Swiftly followed by a second, and then by a third.

The three ships so attacked were in the very forefront of the siege, lined up before the harbor mouth. They burnt like ships of tissue paper soaked in kerosene, and in no time flat were blazing to the waterline.

The Supreme Admiral of All Ziria, Duke Calaphron, confessed himself quite flummoxed by the catastrophe.

Two more ships went up in a sudden, inexplicable blaze.

The High Minister of Ziria, Baron Fraxas, allowed as how he was thoroughly nonplussed by the calamity.

Another Zirian vessel was engulfed in a similar explosion and holocaust.

The Lord General of the Zirian Archers, Count Wuffram, remarked that he would be dad-ratted if he understood what was happening, but ventured to suggest to His Grace the Supreme Admiral that it might be a prudent precaution to command the lead ships to withdraw a mite from the proximity of the sea wall. His Grace drawled that he would take the suggestion under advisement.

Then another ship blew up, and the Duke hastily signalled for the ships of the line to withdraw five hundred yards farther out to sea.

"That may permit the blighters to sail forth and assault us," objected the Baron Fraxas.

"Deuced right, but the blighters are assaultin' us hot and heavy as it is," the Admiral pointed out.

Circling overhead on Ishgadara's back, hidden by the murk from Zirian eyes, Ganelon and Grrff and Zarcas exchanged a satisfied grin as the fleet withdrew to regroup.

It was about time, too. For they were just about out of missiles full of Heek Fire to drop.

If the invading Zirains were mystified by the sudden explosions, the defending buccaneers were positively astounded.

"What in the name of little green fishes is going *on* out there?" muttered Raschid the Red, leaning out of the second-story window with a spyglass clapped to his eye.

"Them ships fum Ziry be a blowin' up, Chief," one of his lieutenants pointed out.

"I can see that, you idiot—but *why?*"

"Beats me, Chief," muttered the officer.

"Well, whatever is happening, it's making the Zirians withdraw to a safer distance. Which gives us a chance to sail out of the harbor," said Raschid with great satisfaction. "Get down there, Skully, and give 'em the word!"

But the remaining Captains of the Bloody Brotherhood did not need official orders to embark. The moment their lookouts announced that the Zirians had withdrawn their line some distance farther out from shore they piled aboard their ships, drew their anchors in, and pointed their prows toward the enemy.

Captains Gronk and Illibus, guarding the sea wall, saw what was happening and ordered the sea chain lowered so as to permit safe passage to the pirate ships.

Ishgadara's artificial feathers were about shot by this time, so she landed her passengers on the deck of the *Bucket o' Blood*, which was already standing to the wind under Squint's command. Zarcas took the helm and followed the ships of Black Horrog and Vlasko and Zollobus out of the harbor.

"Which dew remind me, Capting," whined Squint. "Ol' Raschid, he sent fer yew half a hour ago hit 'twas. Wanted tew see yew up at th' Residence 'bout sumphin."

"Whatever it is, it can wait," said Zarcas.

He was not exactly eager to fight against his own countrymen, and was even more reluctant to slay them. But it seemed likely to the Prince that his old enemy Urzang would be personally commanding the navy of Ziria. The Usurper had slain his father and his brothers, and Zarcas deemed it probable that the villain would be so eager to do in

Zarcas as well that he would, in this instance, overcome his notorious aversion to sea travel in order to be in at the kill.

But Zarcas intended to do the killing. His rapier had been thirsty for the blood of Urzang for ten years.

With luck, it would soon drink deep.

17.

ON THE HIGH SEAS

It was a rather dark night, and what little light came from the star-jeweled skies was lost in the ragged blur of scudding clouds. Through the murk it was only possible to mark the running lights of the enemy ships. These were lanterns of red or green glass, affixed to prow, rudder, mastheads and the like. Guided by these glimmering lamps, the defenders of Arjis Isle steered straight for their adversaries.

Those adversaries, by the way, could discern little in the thick gloom. The reason for this was, quite simply, that the pirates—who had few scruples and even less chivalry—had left their own running lights unlit, the better to confuse the foe.

The foe were quite confused, if not actually alarmed, some little while later when the first of the pirate armada crashed into them. The corsairs struck full on, taking the Zirian galleys broadside, their brazen-beaked prows crunching into the hull timbers. The shock of the collision knocked the Zirian sailors about the decks and they rolled into the scuppers like tenpins. In the next instant, before the dazed, bewildered invaders had struggled to their feet again, grappling hooks swung from piratical hands snagged the reeling ship in a dozen places, holding the two vessels together. Then, raising an unearthly and blood-curdling chorus of vengeful howls and menacing screeches, a flood of wild-eyed buccaneers swarmed aboard and began slaughtering their enemies.

In the gloom it was singularly difficult to tell friend from foe. But the corsairs had each marked out a different ship to assault, ignoring the others. Thus Zarcas, aboard the *Bucket* o' *Blood*, tackled the *Royal* while Horrog, in the *Black Bessie*, directed his own attention against the *Majestic*. At the precise same moment, Vlasko in the *Sea Dog* attacked the *Imperial* and fat Zollobus in the *Red Rover* hurled himself zestfully against the *Fearless*. A tremendous battle ensued, as you might well expect.

The pirates were used to boarding an enemy ship on the high seas, and this attack was not in any particular wise different from many of the others they had initiated. But the Zirian mariners, on the other hand, although well-armed and brave enough, had little if any experience with this variety of war. Confused in the murky darkness, bewildered amid the noise and confusion of struggling men, they were remarkably ineffective. They were also cut down by the score.

The other ships in the huge Zirian fleet stood quite close to their embattled countrymen, but were unable to do very much to help them in their predicament. This was because they were hardly able to see what was going on. From the noise of riot and battle, it was obvious, even to the Zirian officers, that some of their vessels were being attacked—but which *vessels*, and by whom? And where, in all this misty gloom, were they, anyway?

Duke Calaphron, the Supreme Admiral, well aware that his prestige and very reputation hung wobbling in the balance, chafed at the bit. Unable to restrain himself any longer, he directed his flagship against what he thought to be the nearest of the sea vandals. Alas, it was one of his own ships, the unfortunate *Dauntless*, whose running lights had been accidentally extinguished by a gust of spray. But before the Duke discovered his error, he and his men had boarded the *Dauntless*, slaughtered the crew to the last man, and set the ship aflame.

"Tush," exclaimed the Admiral, with a petulant frown. "Dashed bad luck, what?"

He then with his eagle eye spotted another pirate craft by its lean, rakish lines and lack of running lights, and rammed her amidships. This one turned out to be the Zirian carrack *Princely*, under the command of the Zirian High Minister, Baron Fraxas; but the Duke did not find it out until the *Princely* had been sacked and scuttled and his men had brought him the head of the enemy commander, which he easily recognized by its expression of apoplectic fury and pop-eyed outrage.

"Well, 'pon my soul," muttered the Duke absently. "Fraxes, poor blighter! Mention the chap in dispatches. . . ."

The pirates had by this time settled the hash of their respective foes and were zestfully searching out second choices. Horrog directed the *Black Bessie* against the nearest ship, *Valiant,* and Vlasko and Zollobus simultaneously tackled the *Ducal,* but she led them a merry chase. For the high command of the invaders, justifiably alarmed at the rate with which their finest men-of-war were being sunk, decided to pack up and retreat. In no time the enemy fleet had melted into the thick fog and could not be found.

"Suppose we had best mount a vigilant patrol and withdraw to our own harbor and wait for morning," grinned Zarcas the Zirian, well pleased with the manner in which his boys had acquitted themselves.

"That might be best," agreed Ganelon Silvermane, wiping the gore from his silvery broadsword with what had once been a Zirian flag.

"Ya think they're sailin' back to Ziria?" inquired Grrff the Xombolian wistfully. The Karjixian Tigerman had only had—by his standards—a tantalizingly brief taste of combat, and yearned for considerably more.

Zarcas considered briefly, then shook his head.

"I very much doubt it, Sir Grrff," he replied. "They will not have come all this distance to turn back now, after a mere taste of battle. By sunup we shall doubtless mount a pursuit in force . . . and then the pirates of the Bloody Brotherhood shall fight their first sea battle in force!"

This, however, was not to come to pass all that quickly, as things turned out.

Leaving Vlasko and Horrog and two lesser captains to mount sentinel-go before the mouth of the harbor, the defenders of Arjis Isle sailed back to their port. And made haste to report to Raschid the Red.

The Pirate Chief was perplexingly of mixed emotions regarding the victory. On the one hand, he was naturally delighted that his men had so vigorously repulsed the Zirian invasion—even though the fight served to reflect yet more glory and popularity and admiration upon his hated rival, Zarcas. But, on the other hand, he was not happy at the prospects of fighting the Zirian fleet in full force, and by the light of day.

Raschid had a healthy respect for royal navies, and considered, rather disparagingly, that the success his little handful of pirate ships had won against their mightier adversaries was very largely due to the conditions under which the engagement had been fought.

It is one thing to strike at blundering and confused enemies, bewilderedly and half-blindly sailing around in the impenetrable gloom of a cloudy and moonless night. And it is quite another thing to attack a full-sized royal navy by light of day, when they can clearly see you coming.

Raschid, in fine, did not think his men stood a very good chance in a pitched naval battle against the Zirians. They had more ships than he commanded, and larger ones, too. And if Arjis Isle lost her fleet, he would lose his position—not to mention his head.

But he could not very well capitulate to the foe. That would not render him very popular with his corsairs. And they would undoubtedly demonstrate their rancor and disaffection at the ballot boxes in the forthcoming elections . . . and it gnawed at his esteem that his rival Zarcas would undoubtedly reap the benefits of his sharp decline in popularity. . . .

It was the cunning of the Zirian captive, Sir Gyzik, that offered him a prompt and easy solution to his dilemma.

"If the Pirate Chief is wise enough to give the Majesty of Royal Ziria what it wants, methinks the invasion of Isle Arjis and the punishment of the buccaneers could be—ah—postponed. Indefinitely," hissed that sleek and clever villain.

"How's that?" mumbled Raschid.

"All things, in war as in peace, are negotiable," Gyzik reminded the pirate. "Give the Zirians what they want, and I have no doubt that they will sail away with their prize, and leave you in peace to rule your realm."

"Well . . . what do they want?" demanded Raschid.

A wicked gleam flickered in the clever eyes of the spy.

"All they want is one of your captains, the one named Zarcas," he said suavely.

Zarcas!

The solution to Raschid's dilemma was so breathtakingly simple, and so perfect, that the Pirate Chief gasped, blinked dazedly, and licked his thin lips with a pointed tongue, while the same wicked gleam that only a moment before had flickered in Sir Gyzik's eye now glimmered in his own.

How neat and tidy it would be, to solve two problems with the same solution! To get rid of his feared, envied and hated rival—while at the same time getting rid of the enemy fleet without the loss of another piratical life or even the shedding of a single drop more of buccaneer's blood.

It was *so* neat and tidy. . . .

And Raschid liked things to be neat and tidy.

He thought it over, chewing on his lip. The other pirates could certainly not mutter or complain if he ended the war with a single decisive stroke of statesmanship, much as they enjoyed battle.

He rapidly reviewed a mental list of the Council of Captains. Two of them had perished in the siege of Orgaza: Scrimshaw and the fat Clovian, Baba the Barbarous. Scrimshaw was a friend of Zarcas the Zirian, but Baba had been one of Raschid's staunchest supporters and oldest cronies. Of those surviving Captains, only two of the seniormost were of Raschid's party: Skull Wargo and Black Horrog.

But no . . . Skull, that damned fool, had gotten himself rammed, boarded and sunk in the Battle of Orgaza Bay, while locked in an engagement with the Zirian warship *Baronial*. In that contest, *Baronial* had unfortunately emerged the victor.

Which left only Black Horrog. But, luckily, Black Horrog hated and envied the princely young Zirian almost as much as *he* did, Raschid knew. And Horrog ranked Zarcas in the Council, for Zarcas was only the fifth in prestige of the Captains, while Horrog was fourth.

True, the seventh and eighth of the Captains, dour old Vlasko and pudgy, waddling Zollobus, would be vociferous and untiring in their support of the gallant young Zirian. And as for the last two of the Captains, Gronk and Illibis, how they would vote was anybody's guess. The least significant members of the council, they usually kept their mouths shut during the debates and voted with the majority. Still and all, he suspected them of silent Zarcasism.

Raschid chewed his underlip in an agony of indecision. He did not feel that his position was all that secure that he could comfortably turn Zarcas over to the enemy—at least not openly. But something might be arranged. . . .

For the next three days the ships of the Bloody Brotherhood rested in the docks. They were repaired, reprovisioned and made ready to sail. Ishgadara, scouting from the skies, brought back word that the fleet of Ziria had taken refuge to the east and was presently anchored off shore to leeward of the Kakkawakka Isles. The Zirian sailors were also reprovisioning and taking aboard fresh water.

"If we hurry, perchance we can catch them at full anchor,

and under-manned," said Raschid at the emergency Captains'
Council.

"Aye, thet we kin," growled Horrog, glorying in his new
position as Raschid's second-in-command.

Zarcas said nothing; probably because the pirate chief was
right.

"Don't think the fleet can git underway all that fast,
though," said Horrog, who had carefully been coached by his
chief in what to say at the Council and just when to say it.

"Probably not," mused Raschid, making an elaborate
pretense of thinking things over. "However, methinks our gallant Captain Zarcas is ready to sail, and so are our Captains
Vlasko and Zollobus. Is this not so, friends?"

"Aye," nodded Vlasko. Zollobus shrugged. Zarcas indicated
his readiness to sail.

"Then perhaps it would be best to launch an advance
guard to attack and hold the Zirians, until we can follow in
force with the main strength of our fleet," suggested Raschid
cleverly.

No one could find anything wrong with this course of action. It was dangerous, of course, but such as Zarcas and his
friends thrived on danger.

And so it was agreed.

With one addition. Black Horrog would share the honors
of commanding the advance guard in his *Black Bessie*.

And his prisoner would be Sir Gyzik, the Zirian ambassador. For his prisoner's comfort, Horrog was provided with all
sorts of small luxuries.

Even a couple more of those small birds, such as the one
he had dispatched home to Ziria a couple of weeks before,
with a message tied to its foot which had been addressed to
Urzang the Usurper.

On the following morning, the advance guard sailed from
Orgaza Bay, bound for the Kakkawakka Islands.

The ships formed a wedge-shaped sailing order, with Zarcas' own *Bucket o' Blood* in the fore, Horrog's *Black Bessie*
on his starboard and Vlasko's *Sea Dog* on his port side.

Zollobus, in his *Red Rover*, sailed in their wake.

None of them expected anything more than honor, if not
exactly victory.

And none of them was expecting treachery.

Except, of course, for Black Horrog.

18.

LOST AND FOUND

For two full days after leaving the seas around Arjis Isle the expeditionary force sailed due east. By sunset of the third day after leaving the corsair isle they came within sight of their goal. Against a sky of tawny and tangerine flame the Kakkawakkas bulked, black and shaggy.

"Thar they be, awright," observed Squint zestfully. "Ridin' at anchor real peaceful-like, Capting, like as though they ha'nt a enemy in a thousing leagues. . . ."

"Aye," growled One-Eye. "Ripe fer th' pluckin!"

From the masthead, the keenest of eye in all Zarcas' crew was calling down the list of enemy ships.

". . . *Monarchial* . . . *Courageous* . . . *Gallant* . . . *Regal* . . . *Indomitable* . . . nex' one be *Autocratic,* I be thinkin'. . . ." bawled the lookout.

"All ships o' th' line, Cap'n," remarked Claw.

"Mmm," said Zarcas, studying the list. "And there's *Noble,* moored right next to *Baronial.*"

"Warn't hit *Barony* what did fer pore ol' Skull Wargo?" inquired Hook. "Somebody said hit war."

The lookout was still calling off the names of the enemy warships. ". . . *Stalwart* . . . *Kingly* . . . *Honorable,*" he read at intervals. With a slight frown creasing his handsome brow, Zarcas added up the full list.

"Seventeen ships of the line," he reported. "A formidable total, gentlemen . . ."

"Are we gonna fight 'em, or just talk about it?" demanded Grrff the Xombolian, hefting his ygdraxel suggestively.

Zarcas smiled thinly. "We are going to fight them, Sir

144

Grrff," he said. "But using our wits rather than our strength, since in the latter department we seem to be somewhat deficient."

"Remember, if we can see them, they can see us," warned Ganelon Silvermane. Zarcas considered briefly, then shook his head negatively.

"I don't think so, my huge friend," he remarked. "The sunset is behind us, and in order to see us the Zirians must stare directly into the sun. They have no particular reason to believe themselves pursued hither, for if they had they would not all have gone ashore. For, look you, the decks are all but deserted and many bonfires are ablaze upon the beach. No, the Zirians have seized advantage of this respite to try out their land legs again. They have been trading with the savages who infest this isle, and are preparing to enjoy a lazy and drunken feast. With the littlest bit of luck, we can take the rascals by surprise."

Dalassa shivered as if in a sudden chill. "Let's hope for a bit more luck than that," the blonde girl muttered. "With four ships against seventeen, we're gonna need all the luck we can possibly scrounge up!"

Zarcas smiled mysteriously, but said nothing.

He waited for night to fall.

Under cover of darkness the Arjisian flotilla crept in toward the jungle-clad islands. They had of course doused their running lights, and had furled their sails, to boot, in order to present the least visibility possible. On silent wings of tide they glided among the foe.

"Remember, we have only thirty-seven minutes before the Falling Moon will rise," Zarcas warned his men. "So make the best possible use of your time."

"Aye, aye, Capting," grinned Squint. The men set off in longboats, which they rowed with muffled oarlocks. With furtive stealth the boats slid away, vanishing in the darkness. Zarcas himself remained behind, although it irked him not to be able to share the danger with his men. But such, after all, are the responsibilities of command.

By dawn the Zirian lookouts stared—rubbed their eyes unbelievingly—stared again. Then they set up such a clamor that men and officers came scrambling, cursing, staggering out of bed, bunk and hammock, tugging their trousers on and pelting up the stairwells to the decks in record haste.

"Begad," remarked Duke Calaphron, "the blighters are jus'

beggin' t' be hulled. Well, we shall accommodate them, begad!"

Indeed, it seemed to be so. For there in the full light of day the four pirate ships were drawn up at wide intervals, as if for the fray. And the foe wasted precious little time in setting out against them.

That is, they tried to. But something seemed to be the matter; or, rather, several things seemed to be the matter.

For one thing, two of the ships had their anchor chains hopelessly tangled together. These were *Regal* and *Honorable*; and when the seamen, obedient to their officers' commands, strove to reel in the chains, they only dragged the two ships closer together. Finally they collided with a deafening screech and grind of splintering timbers, dislodged masts and crumbling bulwarks. In their confusion the sailors mistook the collision for an attack, and the sailors of *Regal* fell upon the sailors of *Honorable* with brandished cutlasses. A battle royal ensued and it took the better part of an hour for the cursing, perspiring officers to sort everything out.

Autocratic, unable to sail through the two tied-together ships, sought to sail around them, but found her rudder cables had been unfastened and then refastened in reverse. The end result of this was that, instead of sailing out to sea, she turned grandly in toward shore and sank her prow deeply into the sand of the beach. Which was just as well, for by that time the shoals had torn out her hull.

Other ships, their rudder cables sawn through, sailed helplessly around in circles, bumping into each other. It was a scene of indescribable confusion.

"'Pon my word," muttered the Duke through stiff lips. "Deuced mess, what?" With a sinking feeling in his gullet, he tried to imagine what he was going to tell the King of Ziria when he got back home.

If he got back home. . . .

While these things were happening, the pirate ships broke formation and sailed to do battle. They engaged *Baronial* and *Stalwart* but turned aside to avoid the jets of Heek Fire these two galleons directed at them. Next they fell upon the *Brave* and the *Bold*, which were experiencing remarkable difficulties getting under sail. This was because, during the night and under cover of darkness, the buccaneers had tied the ships to rocky outcroppings along the shore. In trying to catch the morning wind, *Brave* broke her keel and *Bold* was straining at the bit (as you might say), but not moving an inch.

Horrog and Zarcas fell upon the two, and boarded them in force.

The only ship not experiencing difficulties was *Dynastic,* which had been skipped the night before, because the pirates were running out of time.

Virtually frothing at the mouth (well, you know what I mean!), *Dynastic* spent most of the morning chasing the smaller, lighter, faster-sailing pirates around the harbor, trying to drive them away from her more-or-less helpless sister ships.

Whenever one of the pirates came within arm's length of the helpless ships, it would have a jet of Heek Fire squirted at it, or a missile lobbed in its direction.

Sometimes this had unhappy results. As, for example, when *Stalwart* fired off a missle of Heek Fire at *Red Rover* but hit poor *Baronial* instead. *Baronial* burst into flames, of course; and so it was that Skull Wargo was avenged.

With her broken keel, *Brave* slowly came apart. By midmorn she was in pieces.

Bold, however, managed to saw through her anchor chain and, once free, sailed forth to engage *Vlasko. Vlasko* turned tail and scooted for the open seas, which was the only thing to do, since *Bold* was twice her size and had twice as many men aboard.

All things considered, it was quite a battle.

By noontime all of the Zirian ships had gotten under sail—those which were still afloat, that is—and all of the pirate ships had sailed out to sea, dispersing according to prearranged plan. Which left the Zirians boiling mad, but with nobody to fight.

By early afternoon the four ships of the pirate flotilla having met at their rendezvouz point, exchanged news.

They also exchanged a roster of the dead or missing.

The very first name on it was that of Zarcas the Zirian.

No one had seen the gallant captain of the *Bucket o' Blood* slain, but he had indeed vanished in the melee. The last anyone had seen of him was when he had gone aboard the *Black Bessie* at Horrog's bequest to attend a captains' conference. Horrog reported that shortly after that they had engaged *Kingly* and that somewhere during the battle Zarcas the Zirian must have fallen overboard, been slain, or perchance taken prisoner. "Mebbe he surrendered," suggested Horrog, with a chuckle and a leer.

"In a pig's eye, he did!" growled Grrff the Xombolian, showing his white teeth in a fearsome grin.

Silvermane also suspected that there was more to this affair than met the eye. Grrff, somewhat blunter and more outspoken, allowed as how he smelled treachery. But there was no proof.

"Something else suspicious," observed Dalassa, her bright eyes mutinous and brighter still with the luster of unshed tears.

"What's that, girl?" demanded the Karjixian Tigerman.

"I thought Raschid was on our very heels with the main fleet," she said tensely. "Well, it's four days now since we set sail out of Orgaźa. And where's Raschid and the fleet?"

Afternoon wore on. They stood out to sea, blocking the Zirian ships from leaving the shelter of the Kakkawakka Islands. Night fell. The pirates maintained roving patrols and mounted alert, well-rested sentries. The Zirians had not moved by dawn.

Nor had Raschid come. . . .

"Treachery it is, then," said Silvermane heavily. It distressed him that True Men could be capable of such wickedness to each other.

That noontime the sailors were getting restless: this stalemate could not last forever. The men drank grog, gambled, swore a lot; they were anxious for some action. And, most likely, the Zirian mariners were in much the same temper. But the enemy ships could not easily sail out of their shelter into the very teeth of the corsairs. They were snug and secure with the Kakkawakka Islands guarding their backs.

After lunch, Kurdi and Zork Aargh joined Grrff at the rail. The boy hung his elbows over the side and bored, kicked at a coil of rope.

"Betcha Cap'n Zarcas is still aboard *Black Bessie*," he said moodily. The Xombolian heaved a sigh.

"You c'd be right, cub," said the Tigerman. "Ol' Grrff's gotta hunch Horrog'd like to git the Cap'n outa th' way. Git him in good with Raschid, that would."

A parley had been announced. In sole charge of the expedition now that Zarcas had so mysteriously vanished, Black Horrog rowed over to Duke Calaphron's flagship in his longboat, bearing a largish chest of—ostensibly—trade goods. Sir Gyzik accompanied him.

When they rowed back, in late afternoon, the chest was conspicuous in its absence. So was Gyzik. And Horrog, of all people, had concluded a peace treaty with the Zirians!

"That blustering idiot wouldn't know a treaty if he fell over one," scoffed Dalassa.

Ganelon frowned, studying a copy. Copies had been distributed among the pirate ships, perhaps to allay suspicions. Puzzle over it as he might, Silvermane could find nothing wrong with it. In return for "certain goods" the Zirian admiral promised to sail the remainder of his fleet back home to Ziria, never to trouble the corsairs of Arjis Isle again, nor even to demand reparations for his losses. It was all very curious. Yet it seemed to hold up under scrutiny.

"Whut 'goods' be them yew guv th' Ziries?" huffed Vlasko suspiciously. Horrog shrugged elaborately, scratching his furry pelt.

"Beads 'n' trinkets 'n' sich-like trash t' trade wif th' natives," said Black Horrog innocently. Nobody was fooled by his meek-as-a-lamb demeanor; on the other hand, there was nothing they could rightly accuse him of.

That evening the pirates rowed ashore under the noses of their former enemies to take aboard fresh supplies of fruit, meat and water. Zork Aargh was among the landing party which set forth from the *Bucket o' Blood*. He did not, however, return with his shipmates.

The plucky little mechanoid was worried that Zarcas had somehow been smuggled aboard the Zirian ships, for it would well have suited Raschid's plans and Horrog's vindictiveness to turn the young corsair over to his most virulent enemies. Such might indeed have been the decisive factor in persuading the Zirians to call off their war.

If his suspicions were correct, then Zarcas was probably by now mewed up in Duke Calaphron's flagship, the *Dynastic*. The galleon was moored offshore, not far out in the harbor, riding up and down at anchor.

Gamely, Zork Aargh waded into the surf. Soon only his head could be espied, bobbing up and down. Presently, it vanished in the seething foam.

Now, the little robot, of course, did not have to breathe in order to sustain his existence, and thus could not possibly drown. About the worst that could happen to him in these circumstances would be that he would leak and blow his batteries. But his bulbous metallic body was well and tightly sealed, and he did not think it very likely.

It was an odd sensation, lumbering along on the sea bottom. It would have been pitch dark by now, had not his triplex eyes cast beams of visible light like miniature searchlights before him, red and yellow and green. Underwater, he discovered, he was almost-but-not-quite weightless: every slow-motion stride made him float off the bottom and slowly drift down again.

The sea bottom was thick with mud and littered with enormous shells, coral branches, boulders. Large, peculiar-looking fish flickered about, eyeing him curiously. Some came so close and got so personal they had to be driven off by flapping his arms.

Before long he found himself under the keel of *Dynastic*. At least, he hoped it was *Dynastic*; in this dim, surreal world of undersea, it was easy to lose your bearings and to confuse your sense of direction.

Zork Aargh kicked free of the mud and floated upwards, waving his four arms like a swimmer. Before long his cylindrical head broke water and he found himself floating on the surface beside a row of portholes. He reached up and caught a ledge of carved and gilded wood, a frieze of dolphins, sea shells and similar nautical motifs.

Moving along this ledge, hand over hand, he negotiated the length of the galleon just above the waterline, peering into each porthole as he passed it.

Some portholes showed sailors snoring in hammocks or dicing by candlelight. Others gave forth on a view of cooks washing up in the galley, officers getting drunk in wardrooms, or dark holds crammed with bales, barrels and boxes.

At long last, one of them revealed a sight which the little mechanoid's triplex optics had long yearned to behold: Zarcas, manacled to rings set in the wall of a cubicle, his blouse in ribbons, but otherwise apparently unharmed. Seated opposite him, with his back to the porthole, was Sir Gyzik. Zorky could not see the spy's face, but felt inwardly certain it wore a self-satisfied smirk.

Still holding onto the ledge with two of his jointed arms, Zork Aargh let go and, with the other two, opened the little storage compartment built in that portion of his anatomy that would have been the tummy of a True Man. He extracted therefrom two power drills.

Working swiftly, he unbolted and screwed off his removable handclamps, and bolted into place and screwed on the two power drills.

Then he set patiently to work cutting through the hull of *Dynastic*.

Directly above his head, Duke Calaphron was taking the

evening air on his quarterdeck. With him was Count Wuf-fram.

"Deucedly calm tonight, what?" remarked the Duke.

"Virtually placid, m'lud," replied the Count.

"Up with the lark tomorrow, Wuffram. Sail home to Ziria, what?"

"Quite right, sir."

"H. M. will be delighted with what we have, ahem, in the aft cargo hold, eh?" snickered the Duke, referring to His Majesty the King of Ziria.

"That he will, m'lud."

On the evening breeze there came to their ears a faint dull drone as of a power drill, or even two, chewing through water-soaked wood.

"Deuced odd. Must be some jungle bird, what?" remarked the Duke, cocking an ear to windward.

"Probably so, sir."

They strolled on, politely smothering their yawns.

19.
PALENSUS CHOY INTERVENES

By morning the sea was filled with ships, and the pirates raised a ragged cheer. For Red Raschid had finally arrived with the full fleet of the Bloody Brotherhood.

Oddly enough, the pirate chief seemed rather disgruntled to observe the stalemate. He sent for Black Horrog without delay. The two conferred in Raschid's cabin, and voices were loudly (if indistinguishably) raised. There were even a few dishes broken, and Horrog emerged from the conference nursing a split lip, a black eye and a lump on his head the size of a nooganooga bird egg.

Negotiations having been completed, the pirate vessels withdrew to permit free passage under truce to the Zirian ships.

The Zirians sailed out of the shelter of the bays and harbors of the Kakkawakka Islands, and promptly fell upon the corsairs. *Dynastic* herself rammed *Black Bessie* at the forefront and set her to the torch.

"What th' blue blazes be goin' on?" demanded Black Horrog bewilderedly, as a swarm of stern-faced Zirians came swinging down through his rigging.

"Cold-blooded treachery, 'pon my word," sniffed Duke Calaphron frostily. The dawnlight gleamed in the mirror of his polished steel cuirass. He set the point of his rapier against Horrog's throat.

"T-t-t-treachery, sez yew?" stammered Horrog confusedly. The poor lout searched his mind, but could think of no particularly treacherous act he had committed. Not lately, that is.

"You sold us the Prince of Ziria," sneered Sir Gyzik from a safe place behind the Duke. "And then you took him back in the night!"

"Divvil a word a truth be in it, Yer Worship," blustered Horrog. But Calaphron was not interested in excuses. He drove his point home, and Horrog fell to the deck, expiring messily.

"Serves me right, I fancy," drawled the Duke, cleaning the gore from his blade by wiping it upon the Admiral's coat Horrog wore. "Nevah deal with th' rabble, don't y'know."

"Words of wisdom, Your Grace," said Gyzik obsequiously. These were, as it turned out, virtually the last words the Zirian spy ever spoke. For, almost immediately, he was set upon by Hookhand and Zilch, first and second mates respectively to the late Horrog. These worthies viewed the dispatching of their former captain with commendable displays of righteous fury, and leaped upon the Duke and Gyzik, voicing loud squawks of rage and dismay.

Calaphron snapped down his visor and retreated, quite sensibly, into the refuge of his plate armor. Gyzik wore only a corselet, and retired in all haste, squeaking and begging mercy.

He received none. But he did get a cutlass through the middle which quite effectively cost the Zirian Espionage Corps its star employee.

Shortly thereafter the battle became chaotic and unruly, and the Duke sensibly retired to the relative safety of his own quarterdeck, there to more ably direct the fighting.

Black Bessie burned to the waterline, but Zilch and Hookhand led most of their shipmates to safety.

Words cannot adequately describe the outrage and fury Red Raschid displayed, learning that all his cunning and carefully laid plans had gone awry. To say that he actually foamed at the mouth and broke a tooth on his own bronze astrolabe is to be guilty of understatement. (He broke two.)

For Zarcas, miraculously, had turned up not only still alive but free and aboard his own ship. This was Zork Aargh's doing, as you and I know, but Raschid knew only that everything had gone wrong. And he had sailed into the very midst of a major sea engagement unwittingly. It was the last thing he desired; but there was no getting out of it now.

And so the Battle of the Kakkawakkas ensued. It was very long and very bloody and very complicated. So complicated that I will not bore my readers with a blow-by-blow (or even a ship-by-ship) account of the fray. Suffice it to say that the

Arjis Islanders lost Horrog's *Black Bessie* and three lesser ships, while the Royal Zirian Navy lost *Stalwart, Regal* and *Courageous.* ·

Raschid performed prodigies of seamanship; time and again his captaincy and shrewd oversight led him to the rescue of one or another of his vessels. A consummate villain he certainly was; but it came as something of a surprise to Silvermane, Grrff, Dalassa and our other friends to discover that he was also a consummate commander as well.

Grrff and Silvermane did what little they could do in the battle, but their skills were primarily those of the land, not of sea warfare. Dalassa and Kurdi and little Zork Aargh kept out of the way as much as possible. Ishgadara flew reconnaissance missions until her wings were weary. But it all came to naught, or seemed as if that's where it would come in the end.

For there were, quite simply, a lot more Zirian ships than Arjisian; and in a sea battle, numbers count for a lot.

One of the Arjisian ships, *Skull an' Crossbones,* was boarded by assault parties from *Knightly,* and the officers of the pirate ship were slaughtered to the last man. As it happened, this was the ship that had taken aboard the survivors of Horrog's *Black Bessie,* so Hookhand and Zilch assumed command and turned on *Knightly* and gave it back in her very teeth.

Knightly was too big for them to take, but it pleased Zilch in particular that she turned and ran from them.

Both Vlasko and Zollobus performed prodigies in turn; but prodigies were only to be expected from the two old comrades, and were not to be remarked upon.

Ishgadara dropped missiles of Heek Fire upon *Staunch* and she blew up. Those being the last of the Heek Fire missiles Arjis Isle had, the wing-weary sphinx-girl retired to the hold of Zarças' ship, curled up on a pile of canvas, and requested Claw to wake her when it was all over.

Dynastic, having sunk two pirate ships in turn, directed her efforts against Raschid in his *Sea Dragon.* Zarcas, realizing that the Raschid's galley was no match against the Admiral's flagship, sped to her rescue.

At the identical moment, *Noble, Indomitable* and *Kingly* sailed against the wind, tacking about to block Zarcas from aiding his Chief.

"Here hit comes, big man," groaned Grrff. "Three a them great warships. . . . We ain't gotta chance. An t' think, ol' Grrff allers wantid t' die on dry land—!"

"Courage," rumbled Silvermane, "the battle is not yet lost."

"Our part of it is," grunted the Tigerman.

And then the world went dark.

Everybody looked up quickly.

Above them, floating weightless as a cloud against the blue sky, hovered an enormous castle of white, glittering stone. It was built on a square, solid base, all of one piece, ringed about with a wall and spired with towers and turrets.

Although it must have weighed many thousands of tons, it drifted as lightly as a soap bubble on the breeze.

The pirates, the Zirians, and whatever Kakkawakka Islanders happened to be watching, had no notion of what it was, nor of how or why it had come there. To say that they were dumbfounded would be putting it mildly: they were petrified.

Ganelon and his companions, however, recognized the fantastic structure as Zaradon, the famous Flying Castle which belonged to their old friend, Palensus Choy, the Immortal. They raised a hearty cheer and began waving their weapons, or (in Ishgadara's case) their wings.

The Flying Castle settled downward with great deliberateness. And, unfortunately, *Dynastic* was directly underneath the castle's base. And when several thousand tons of solid castle decide to sit down on a warship, that warship had best be stricken from the naval rolls.

It cracked open like an egg; pressed down under the water, it flooded and sank with a horrendous gurgling sound.

Then everything began to happen at once.

Raschid's *Sea Dragon*, which had been in the process of coming about into the wind to face it out with *Dynastic*, ran smack into Zaradon's wall. The screech of tortured, splintering timbers was deafening.

The Zirian ships *Noble*, *Indomitable* and *Kingly*, which had been in pursuit of Zarcas, veered off to either side frantically, rather than approach in proximity to the flying stone monster. They ran into each other, and, a few minutes later, rising with stately and dignified grandeur out of the water, Zaradon sat down on them for good measure.

Dictatorial and *Monarchial* attempted to attack the Flying Castle. They tacked about. Catapults whanged. Missiles whizzed through the air. Explosions of Heek Fire flared against the walls of Zaradon. They smoked and sizzled for a time, then spluttered out, leaving nasty great black stains against the snowy, sparkling walls.

The two ships retired in confusion. Looking about, their

captains could perceive only four other Zirian ships that still happened to be afloat.

The total was not particularly inspiring. Neither was it conducive to valor in the teeth of such opposition.

White flags blossomed, one by one, from the six Zirian mastheads.

And the Battle of the Kakkawakkas was at an end.

Longboats were launched to pluck any survivors from the drink. Signal flags fluttered up the lines, giving the tally. *Sea Dragon* had sunk with all hands, and Raschid the Red was no more. As senior surviving member of the Captains' Council, Zarcas was now in full command of the Arjisian fleet.

Flying a flag of truce from his masthead, he sailed alongside the Flying Castle, which was hovering a dozen yards above the tangled wreckage of the three Zirian galleons it had recently squashed.

Three human figures appeared atop Zaradon's wall. Well, actually, only two of them were human, for the other was Chongrilar the Stone Man. But the two that were not of stone were indisputably human, although quaint in their appearance.

One of them was lean and lanky, with a long beard, a purple gown, and an expression of benign and affable abstraction on his features. This was the distinguished immortal magician, Palensus Choy.

His companion was as short and broad and belligerent as Choy was tall, slender and benign. He had a fat-cheeked face, quite red, very bald, and adorned with mustachios of heroic proportions. This was the distinguished machinist, tinkerer and inventor, Ollub Vetch.

They waved.

Zarcas, arrayed in his most magnificent peach-and-bronze satin, climbed into the fo'castle and called up through a paper trumpet.

"Ahoy, the castle! Permission to come aboard?"

Choy nodded absently.

"By all means, my dear fellow . . . you'll be just in time for tea."

Ishgadara flew them up to the top of the wall, making two trips to ferry all of the principals aloft. Once they had dismounted, they all greeted one another, Dalassa with considerable curiosity, and Zork Aargh with extreme timidity.

Kurdi, of course, flung himself squealing upon the tall magician and the stubby little inventor, neither of whom he had seen for the better part of two years. They patted him, hugged him, and marveled at the way he had grown.

Grrff and Silvermane shook hands heartily with their two famous friends, and demanded to know how they had come in the veritable nick of time. The last they had seen of the duo had been during the Great Ximchak Migration about two years before.*

Palensus Choy stroked his beard absently, and murmured: "Well, my dear Silvermane, you know that our agreement with that ruffian, Wolf Turgo, forbade our interfering with the Ximchaks any further. So Vetch and I remained in Gompland, helping with the famine and all of that sort of thing."**

"Yes, I remember," nodded Silvermane. "How are all the Gomps, anyway?"

"Doing as well as may be expected. With our, ah, aid they survived the winter and that dreadful famine. Princess Ruzara's sister has turned out to possess an admirable grasp of administrative technique . . . and how is Ruzara, anyway, may I inquire? I perceive that she is no longer with you. . . ."

Grrff grinned. "Settled down with Harsha o' th' Horn 'an' got spliced up in th' Merdingian Regnate," he chuckled. "Gotta litter o' cubs by now, ol' Grrff guesses!"

"Indeed," murmured Choy vaguely, "fancy that!"

"As you were saying," said Ganelon patiently.

"Oh, yes, of course! Dear me, how forgetful I am becoming. . . . Well, from time to time we, ah, looked in on you through my magic crystal, just to keep, ah, tabs on how you were doing . . . most recently, Ollub Vetch reminded me that dear Ishgadara was still missing from the Menagerie, so we, ahem, tuned in on your affairs. Well, we were quite surprised to find you all the way down here in Lower Arzenia, pottering about the Zelphodon with all of these distressing corsairs. So we decided to pay you a visit, and seem to have arrived in the midst of a naval engagement of sorts. I, ah, *do*

* Ibziz' Commentary on the Epic remarks at this point that it had been *exactly* one year, seven months and fourteen days since Ganelon and his companions had bade farewell to Zaradon at the Hills of the Strange Little Men. Ibziz was always a stickler for accuracy and I am too busy to figure out if his math is correct.
** The incident to which Choy refers may be found in the concluding chapters of the Third Book of the Epic, *The Immortal of World's End.*

hope our intervention was apt and timely, however inadver-.
tent?"

"It was," said Silvermane.

Just then Ishgadara came flapping down to deposit her
second party load of passengers atop the parapet. These
consisted of the Grand Magnate Borgo Methrix, who had followed Raschid's fleet all the way from Arjis aboard the *Pride
of Urgoph*, Zork Aargh, Zarcas the Zirian, and—by way of
an unexpected surprise—Duke Calaphron of Ziria, still dripping messily. He had swum ashore, been captured by the
Kakkawakka savages, purchased his freedom by giving the Islanders all of his jeweled orders, badges and other accouter-
ments, up to and including his diamond-studded monocle.

Then he had been captured all over again by the pirates.
He looked considerably crestfallen, as might any Admiral
who had suffered so devastating a defeat.*

Ganelon introduced the Grand Magnate of Urgoph, the
True Heir of Ziria, and the waterlogged Duke to their hosts.

Clucking sympathetically over Calaphron's bedraggled appearance, Palensus Choy bade Chongrilar the Stone Man
draw a hot bath for the peer and lay out fresh clothing.

As for the fat little inventor, he had eyes for none but
Zork Aargh. A predatory gleam in his eye, Ollub Vetch
waddled quickly over and began looking the mechanoid up
and down with approval.

"Valdalexian work, aren't you, me bucko?" he inquired,
rapping Zorky here and there on various portions of his
metallic anatomy.

"Yes, please," clicked the small robot apprehensively.

"Fine work they did, those Technarchs," sighed Vetch.
"Come down to me workshop, little feller, and I'll check out
yer oil."

They waddled off together.

Palensus Choy had by now been introduced to Calaphron,
Zarcas, Borgo Methrix and Dalassa, had shaken hands with
Grrff and Ganelon, had been hugged by a delighted Kurdi,
and had patted a grinning, tongue-lolling Ishgadara.
Scratching the Gynosphinx behind the ears and looking
around absently, the Magician of Zaradon cleared his throat.

"Well, now that we are all here and the social amenities

---

* Of the thirty-two warships which had comprised the Zirian naval expedition against the pirates, only six vessels were still afloat. For the
statistic I am again indebted to the estimable Ibziz.

are cleared away," he suggested, "I suspect that you would all enjoy a good luncheon."

They heartily agreed, and trooped down into the castle hall for one of Chongrilar's succulent repasts.

20.

HAIL AND FAREWELL

Dalassa found luncheon in Castle Zaradon a feast sumptuous even by the standards of Urgoph: there was braised unicorn liver in yikkleberry sauce, candied butterflies, tender lux cutlets in cream gravy, and broth of sea serpent with croutons, not to mention delicious Kakkawakka Island salad. Chongrilar had truly outdone himself this time.

Over hot junglefruit turnovers, fayowaddy tea and flowerseed cakes, they all vied with each other in telling the story of their recent adventures. Silvermane solemnly recounted how he had gained mastery of the Ximchak Barbarians and led the Horde north and west into Upper Arzenia all the way to Merdingia, where the Horde had gradually dispersed.

Kurdi (with many promptings from Grrff, mostly of a grammatical nature) then told how the three of them, mounted on Ishgadara, had journeyed south to Soorm and Urgoph. At that point Grrff explained how they had destroyed the Talking Heads, beaten off the Arjisian invasion, and been carried off by the pirates. In turn, Zarcas told of their voyage to Arjis Isle, Borgo Methrix related the tale of his own voyage to the pirate kingdom to ransom his daughter and her friends, and Zork Aargh explained how he had joined them at Korscio.

Then it was the reluctant turn of Duke Calaphron, with many ahems and harrumphs, to tell how the spy Gyzik had sent a secret message back to Ziria informing Urzang the Usurper of the existence of the exiled heir to the Zirian throne, of the naval expedition against Arjis Isle, and of the three battles wherein that expedition had been decimated.

All in all, it was quite a story, and it took the lot of them most of the afternoon to tell it.

Choy, for his part, gave a meandering account of how the starving Gomps had survived the winter with help from Trancore and other neighbors, and how splendidly Princess Mavella, Ruzara's sister, was doing as the new Plutarchus Regina of Gompery.

Twilight had fallen before all of the stories had been completely told. Grrff, Ganelon, Kurdi and Ishgadara spent the night in their old apartments in the Flying Castle, but Zarcas and his prisoner the Duke returned to the *Bucket o' Blood*, while Dalassa and Borgo Methrix slept in the *Pride of Urgoph*.

Zork Aargh, who never slept anyway, stayed up all night conversing with Chongrilar the Stone Man and being introduced by Ishgadara to the various fabulous creatures who lived in the menagerie of Palensus Choy.

The next morning Zarcas permitted Duke Calaphron and the remants of his fleet to depart for Ziria. He did not even bother to require a nonaggression pact from the Zirian admiral, knowing that King Urzang would immediately repudiate any such treaty as soon as he heard of it. The pirates were a trifle disgruntled that their commander was not going to scuttle the six remaining Zirian warships and hold their crews and the survivors of the other ships for ransom, but Zarcas firmly explained that they would have to feed, clothe and house the Zirians, and that Urzang probably wouldn't foot the bill in any case.

Then the pirate fleet prepared to sail back to Arjis Isle. The return voyage took three days, and Zaradon accompanied the fleet all the way, floating overhead like some remarkable geometrical cloud.

Once back in their stronghold, the pirates prepared to elect their new Chief. It was a trifle early for the elections, but since the office had been left vacant by the demise of Raschid, the Articles of the Bloody Brotherhood demanded elections be held instantly.

Of course, Zarcas the Zirian was swept into office by an overwhelming majority of the votes. Not only was he the seniormost of the Captains left alive, but his prestige had grown enormously by his valor in the recent battles against the Zirians. A week after their return, he was inaugurated and moved into the Residence with all ceremony.

His first official acts were to negate the ransom demands

against Borgo Methrix and to give the *Pride of Urgoph* the
freedom of the seas.

He then signed a treaty with Urgoph, rendering Urgovian
shipping forever immune to piratical depredations. The treaty
required that a diplomatic representative of Urgoph remain
in residence at Arjis; this—to no one's particular surprise—
turned out to be Dalassa.

The blonde girl went pink to the hairline at the knowing
chuckles and smirks that went around when it became known
that she would remain indefinitely oh Arjis. Not even the
lowliest cook or cabinboy among the pirates but was fully
aware that she and the new pirate chief were in love.

During the next three days, Zarcas moved to bring the
Council of Captains up to its required number of ten. His old
friends Vlasko and Zollobus were elevated to the second and
third place in the Council, and Gronk and Illibis were also
moved up. The other vacancies on the Council were filled by
Zilch and Hookhand, Horrog's mates, who had performed
gallantly in the Battle of the Kakkawakkas and were, anyway, long overdue for ships of their own to command.

His own mates, Squint and Claw, were awarded captaincies
in honor of their faithful service and superior seamanship.
The skinny Ikzikian allowed as how he would be blowed at
the news, and blew his pointed yellow nose vigorously into a
pocket handkerchief, declaring moistly that he must be
catching a cold.

As for Claw—or Captain Uxab, as he was henceforward to
be known—the supercrustacean swelled visibly with pride,
and assumed at once a lordly, aloof manner.

But it did not go unnoticed that the two former mates of
the *Bucket o' Blood* sneaked away from the ceremony as
soon as they could decently do, and scurried off to inspect
their new ships, left masterless through losses suffered in the
recent battle.

As for the tenth vacancy on the Council, it was awarded to
none other than Ganelon Silvermane. Which came as an
amazing surprise to that worthy, but to no one else who had
observed him in action at the Battles of Orgaza or the
Kakkawakkas.

Somewhat flustered, Silvermane explained that he did not
think he would be staying very long at Arjis Isle, but would
be moving on. Zarcas grinned, clapped him on the shoulder,
and said that the captaincy, in that case, would be an honorary one. For so long as the young giant wished to dwell in
the pirate kingdom, he would command the good ship *Scarlet*

Cutlass; and if and when he wished to move on to other adventures in far lands, he would forever retain his captaincy as a perpetual honor.

Ganelon confessed himself to be deeply touched. And privately resolved to change the name of his new command to the *Honor of Zermish*, which he soon did.

And he too departed the festivities as soon as was decent, to inspect the vessel that now was his. Growing up in Zermish, he had thrilled over swashbuckling tales of piratical adventure on the High Seas: and now he, himself, was actually a pirate!

Not every boy grows up to live his own dreams. Ganelon was one of the lucky ones. . . .

Three days after this, Palensus Choy and Ollub Vetch announced that it was time for them to take their departure. It was their intention to fly Zaradon home to her old, familiar perch atop Mount Naroob, from which she had been absent now for some years.

A few years, of course, are as nothing to the life of one such as Palensus Choy, whose longevity was remarkable.* But magicians, on the whole, are a quiet, peaceable, law-abiding folk, who like a snug castle far from the hurlyburly, wherein to conduct their interminable studies and experiments. And excitement and adventure and foreign travel, while stimulating, wear after a while on those of scholarly temperament.

Ganelon, Grrff and Kurdi were sad to bid their old friends farewell, for they had shared many exciting times together in Trancore and Valardus and Kan Zar Kan. But they knew the absent-minded sorcerer and his plump inventor-friend yearned for some quiet times at Naroob after all these adventures.

"You must all come to Zaradon someday for a visit," said Choy with just the hint of a quaver in his reedy voice. "For we shall miss you, and will always be delighted to see you again."

"Aye, an' that goes fer me, too," said Ollub Vetch, striving to swallow the lump in his throat.

They shook hands solemnly.

Perhaps the worst would be parting from Ishgadara. Silvermane and his companions had shared so many experiences with the friendly, cheerful, resourceful sphinx-girl, that it

---

* The famous Immortal of Zaradon was then some six and one-half million years old, which would be remarkable in any epoch.

would be difficult to do without her invaluable presence on whatever adventures lay ahead for them.

And she was sad, too, at the thought of saying good-bye. But she was homesick for her cozy stall in Choy's menagerie of magical mythical beasts, and longed to renew her acquaintance with her old friends Harooshk the Mandragon, the Great White Youk Eezik, Thurble the Pyrosprite, the Mantichore Jrngka, and Orillibis the enormous Piast.

Also, she explained shamefacedly, blubbering just a little through her good-byes, Gynosphinxes (and, as far as that goes, Androsphinxes, too), moult and hibernate every lustrum. And, as the five-year-period was by now just about up, Ishgadara was getting a bit sleepy.

The farewells were hardest of all, I suppose, on Kurdi. Ganelon and Grrff and Ishgadara were all the family the young boy had ever known. Especially Ishgadara.

He flung his brown arms around her huge neck and hugged her with all his might, snuffling and weeping into her curly mane, while she grinned and blinked back tears and patted him clumsily with feather-soft taps of her enormous paws.

"Oh, Ishy, I'm going to miss you," he sobbed.

"Ishy knowingk that," she said softly. "Ishy goingk to miss Kurdi, too. Maype I comingk to visit you, sometime. . . ."

"Oh, will you, *really?*"

She nodded. Then she yawned vastly, revealing rows of blunt white tushes.

"Put now me gettingk sleepy," she murmured drowsily.

That afternoon, the Flying Castle rose lightly from the beach beyond Orgaza, flew in a wide circle around the town with all pennants fluttering from her spires, and vanished in the blue distance.

Grrff, Ganelon, Kurdi and the others waved good-bye from the roof of the Residence so long as the smallest white fleck of white was still visible against the sky. Then they went in to supper.

And, who knows, perhaps they would meet again, somewhere in the future.

Partings between dear and close friends are seldom forever.

It was three months to the day since they had awoken in the Desolation of Oj to discover Kurdi missing, to rescue Dalassa from the Deacons, and to begin getting involved in the fortunes of Urgoph, Soorm, Arjis Isle and Ziria. This thought occurred to Grrff the Xombolian after dinner, while toasting his toes before a roaring fire in the little harbor-front inn where he and Silvermane had taken quarters.

So much had happened to them during the past ninety days . . . so many new friends (and enemies) had they made, so many strange cities, islands and countries had they visited, so many invasions, battles and engagements had they fought. . . .

Grrff reflected drowsily that it was odd, in a way, that so much can happen to a person in so little time.

He also mused, with a grin of relish, over how much had happened to him since he first met up with Ganelon Silvermane, nearly three years before.*

He had been arrested, captured, kidnapped, almost sacrificed, and very nearly slain more times than he could possibly count. And he had met kings, emperors, knaves, savages, pirates, knights, wizards, robots, dukes, princesses, spies, thieves, inventors, gypsies, intelligent cities, stone men, talking monsters, barbarians and soldiers. He had even met a Dragon that was the Oldest Thing in the World.

He had crossed deserts, mountains, seas, forests, swamps, jungles, and more kingdoms and countries than he could begin to remember.

Somehow or other, he had heartily enjoyed all of it. Well . . . *almost* all of it. Enough, at any rate, to have made the whole thing worthwhile. And when, if ever, he finally got back home to Xombol in Karjixia, he would be known as the most traveled of all his fellow Tigermen in their long and vivid history.

It had all been quite an adventure, now that he thought of it.

He yawned hugely, displaying snowy fangs.

The wine bottle, he noticed, was empty.

"Guess I'll go to bed now, Grrff," said Ganelon from the other chair, stretching his mighty arms.

"Um."

"Got to be up early tomorrow morning, you know," said the other. Which reminded Grrff, now the first mate of the *Honor of Zermish* and a pirate of the Bloody Brotherhood,

---

* According to the invaluable Ibziz and his chronology of the Epic, exactly two years, ten months and nineteen days had elapsed between the day Grrff and Ganelon first met in the arena at Shai and this scene. Or 1039 days, if you prefer.

that on the morrow they intended to take the ship out on a shakedown cruise. He blinked sleepily into the fire.

"Guess ol' Grrff'll be gittin' t' bed, too," said Grrff the Xombolian.

They left the room together.

Appendix

**A Glossary of Places
Mentioned in
The Text**

A GLOSSARY OF PLACES
MENTIONED IN THE TEXT

Note: All place names thus far listed in the first five books of the Epic are listed here in the three portions of my glossary; they include the names of such natural features as deserts, mountains, forests, seas, rivers and so on, plus all man-made structures and political divisions, as cities, towns, kingdoms, empires, etc. The Roman numeral following each entry signifies the volume of the Epic wherein primary mention is made of that entry: I. refers to *The Warrior of World's End*, II. *The Enchantress of World's End*, III. *The Immortal of World's End*, IV. *The Barbarian of World's End*, and V. *The Pirate of World's End*. The Arabic numeral which follows the Roman identifies the specific chapter of each book in which the primary mention appears.

Realm of the Nine Hegeomons, The. *See* The Hegemony.
Renoza. One of the many streams in Malme River Country. IV, 17.
Ridonga. Site of the School of the Sixty Sciences (See Nembosch.) I, 11.
Rith River Country. A region in Greater Zuavia. III, 18.
Rlambar Mountains. A range which forms the borders of the Plains of Vlith. IV, 12.
Romode. A lake near Xombol in Karjixia. I, 21.
Rosch. A City in Gompland. III, 18.
Ruggosh. A region in Greater Zuavia which includes Rith River Country and the Five Towns of Xarge. III, 18.
Runcy. Town in Southern YamaYamaLand. V, 5.
Ruxor. The famous Petrified City on the Plains of Vlith. IV, 12.

Sabdon. Northernmost of the cities of the Hegemony. I, 3.

Sargish. Capital of Pardoga. IV, 14.

Serrium. One of the Deserted Cities in Malme River Country seized by the Scavengerlike Voygych River Brigands. IV, 16.

Shai. Capital of the Land of Red Magic north of the Hegemony. II, 8.

Shu. The region beyond the mountains, north of Sargish. IV, 15.

Shyx. Meadowlands east of the Luzar Pass in Greater Zuavia. III, 9.

The Singing River. Exactly what it sounds like, and in Greater Zuavia. III, 17.

Sky Island. An island suspended in midair above the earth over Karjixia. Formerly the haunt of the rapacious Airmasters. I, 18.

The Sleeping Forest. A tract in Pardoga placed under an enchantment by Uxorian Maximus. IV, 31.

The Smoking Mountains. Volcanic Range of active volcanoes in Southern YamaYamaLand. I, 1.

Soorm. A land near Urgoph on the North Shore of the Zelphodonian Sea, famous for its Talking Heads. V, 4.

Sorabdazon. A region in Upper Arzenia from which the Pardogamen fled to escape the Green Wraiths. IV, 13.

Southern YamaYamaLand. The Conglomerate from which Phlesco and Imminix hale. It is the scene of the Sixth Book of the Epic. I, 1.

Spoyda. A city in the Merdingian Regnate, ruled by the Marquis Ferrule. IV, 19.

Tabernoy. City of Atheists. III, 17.

Thash. A river in Pardoga. IV, 14.

Thazarian Mountains, The. A range which borders on Karjixia to the south; site of the famous Air Mines. I, 18.

Thoph. Central island in the Cham Archipelago. II, 18.

Thu Mountains. A range which borders on the Fire Desert of Xoroth to the north; beyond them lies the land of the Warrior Women of Khond. IV, 12.

Thundermountains Falls. A famous cataract on the North Shore of the Sea of Zelphodon, where the Zelphus River flows into the inland sea. I, 3.

Thunder Troll Mountain. Tallest and most prominent of the Embosch Mountains which separate Gompland from the Mad Empire. IV, 1.

Torx. A small kingdom in Upper Arzenia, narrowly missed by the Great Ximchak Migration. IV, 21.

Trancore. An island and a city in the Greater Pommernarian Sea; site of the Mad Empire of Trancore, ruled by the Gray Dynasts. III, 18.

The Triple City. A triune metropolis, composed of the cities of Hylage, Janeel and Korascio. IV, 16.

Tucsan Mountains. A range in Upper Arzenia, south of Volesce. V, 1.

Ubbolon. A river in Pardoga. IV, 14.

Uchamboy. A region in Southern YamaYamaLand, site of the famous Carved Cliffs. IV, 16.

Ulkh. A section of the river Kurge where dangerous rapids make the stream difficult to negotiate. V, 1.

Upper Arzenia. A Conglomerate due west of Greater Zuavia; therein lie Pardoga, Malme River Country and the Merdingian Regnate. IV, 12.

Urchak. Jungle town, capital of Nimboland. III, 8.

Urd. A city in the Merdingian Regnate. IV, 19.

Urgoph. Seaport city on the North Shore of Zelphodon; an oligarchy like Gompland, ruled by the Grand Magnate. V, 3.

Urimadon. Whatever it is, it lies west of the Crystal Mountains. I, 4.

Uroph. A city in Malme River Country, inhabited only by Voygych. IV, 16.

The Urrach. A forested tract near Trancore on the Ovarva Plains. III, 24.

Uskodian Plains, The. Region near Pardoga; also the name of a range of mountains there. IV, 12.

Uth. Dried riverbed in the Plains of Uth, west of Zermish. I, 6.

Valardus. Kingdom situated at the southern terminus of the Luzar Pass through the Carthazian Mountains, where the pass opens upon the Purple Plains. IV, 2.

Vandalex. Extinct civilization prominent in a former eon, that of the Flying Cities. The Technarchs of Vandalex were responsible for many of the scientific marvels thus far encountered in the Epic, such as the Mobile City of Kan Zar Kan and the friendly mechanoid, Zork Aargh. Silvermane does not visit the ruins of Vandalex (more properly, of its capital, Grand Phesion) until the Eighth Book.

Vanishing Mountains, The. A range which sometimes exists between Chx and the country of the Death Dwarves—and sometimes does not. II, 6.

Vemblem. A town in Upper Arzenia. V, 1:

The Vermilion Marshes. Whatever they are, they are also in Upper Arzenia, and extremely Red. V, 1.

Vigola Pass, The. A northern pass through the Embosch Mountains; thereby Ganelon Silvermane led the Ximchaks out of Gompery. IV, 11.

Vlad. Fourth largest of the inland seas of Gondwane the Great. III, 18.

Vladium. Capital of Jemmerdy. I, 20.

Vlith. Meadowlands beyond the Hu Pass through the Rlambars. IV, 12.

Volesce. The town near the Tucsan Mountains where the adventurers spent the winter before venturing south to Soorm and Urgoph. V, 1.

Voorm. About twenty-five thousand years ago, the Lost Sea of Voorm occupied much of Northern YamaYamaLand. It was the largest of all of the inland seas of Gondwane. III, 18.

The Voormish Desert. Sandy tract north of the Crystal Mountains; once the floor of the Lost Sea of Voorm, now inhabited mostly by Nomad tribes descended from the Sea Barbarians who had sailed the Lost Sea in primal epochs. I, 15; III, 18.

The Warbird Cliffs. A narrow pass in Upper Arzenia, beyond the Triple City, walled with cliffs whose niches are the lairs of carnivorous birds. Ganelon led the Ximchaks through this dreadful gamut. IV, 16.

Warwhith. A city in the Gompish Regime. III, 18.

The Warza. A forested tract west of the Plains of Uth. I, 5.

Warzoon. The famous city of the magicians in Upper Arzenia north of Pardoga. IV, 14.

Wazuzu. The city in which Jingoism arose. III, 9.

West Rlambar Mountains. The branch of the Rlambars which forms the western borders of Pardoga and Vlith. IV, 12.

White Waste, The. A wilderness region south of the Merdingian Regnate, infested by the Vroych. V, 1.

Wryneck River. Its source is in the Embosch Mountains of Greater Zuavia, and it empties into the Greater Pomernarian Sea. III, 21; IV, 2.

Xarge. A confederation of five towns in Ruggosh. III, 10.

Xim River. In the remote northern parts of Gondwane the Great, in the plains between the rivers Xim and Chak, once dwelt the nomadic ancestors of the Ximchak Horde. IV, 19.

Xombol. Capital of Karjixia and birthplace of Grrff. I, 21.

Xor. A lake in Greater Zuavia near the Arzenian border. Pathon Thad is in its center. IV, 12.

Xorish River. It rises north of Qoy and empties into Lake Xor. IV, 12.

Xoroth. Name of the Fire Desert east of the Gompish Regime. IV, 7.

Xuru Pass. A way through the northern Embosch Mountains by which the Ximchaks entered Gompery. IV, 1.

Yadder Hills. The hills overlook Spoyda in Merdingia, and "yadder" is a color invisible to our eyes but visible by Ganelon's time. IV, 19.

Yellow Hills. Hills near Luzzuma in the Gompish Regime. IV, 7.

Yembar Chasm. A cleft in the Crystal Mountains. I, 12.

Yombok. A country north of Quay and Karjixia, famous for its white-eyed witches. I, 4.

Zaim Rock. An eminence in Uth where the Zermishmen were ambushed by Indigons. I, 5.

Zaradon. The famous Flying Castle of Palensus Choy, usually (but not always) situated atop Mount Naroob in the Iriboth Mountains. III, 10.

Zarge. A country north of Malme River Country to which the Malmian Dynasts fled. They were great builders, it is thought, and could not endure living any longer in Malme within sight of the devastatingly superb sculptures of the Marvelous Mountains. IV, 16.

Zermish. Westernmost of the nine cities of the Hegemony; therein Ganelon Silvermanè was raised by his foster parents, Phlesco and Imminix, and spent his early years. I, 1-7.

Zelphodon. The third lesser inland sea of Gondwane, situated partly in Lower Arzenia spilling over into Southern YamaYamaLand in its eastern parts. V, 7 *etc.*

Zelphus River. With the Kurge, the major affluent of the Zelphodonian Sea. The Zelphus is in Southern YamaYamaLand and rises in the foothills of the Smoking Mountains. I, 3.

Zingaree. An atoll in the Sea of Zelphodon. V, 9.

Ziria. Homeland of Captain Zarcas. V, 12.

Zuav River. Two and one half million years before Ganelon's time the founders of Greater and Lesser Zuavia came from their mythic homeland on the shores of this river in the north. II, *Appendix,* "Greater Zuavià."

Zyle. The Isle of Zyle lies in the Sea of Zelphodon. V, 4.

Zynor Island. An islet in the Kurge. V, 1.

CPSIA information can be obtained
at www.ICGtesting.com
Printed in the USA
LVOW07s0750130717
541192LV00001B/7/P